The Bone Seekers

Les chercheurs d'os

Tahar Djaout

TRANSLATED BY

Marjolijn de Jager

DIÁLOGOS BOOKS

DIALOGOSBOOKS.COM

ii

The Bone Seekers
an English translation of *Les chercheurs d'os.*
by Tahar Djaout
Translated by Marjolijn de Jager

Printed in the U.S.A.
First Printing
10 9 8 7 6 5 4 3 2 1   18 19 20 21 22 23

Book and Cover design: Bill Lavender

Library of Congress Control Number: 2018946911
Djaout, Tahar
The Bone Seekers / Tahar Djaout
with Marjolijn de Jager, translator
p. cm.
ISBN: 978-1-944884-49-9
EBook: 978-1-944884-50-5

DIÁLOGOS BOOKS
DIALOGOSBOOKS.COM

Acknowledgments

The translator would like to express her sincere appreciation to Peter Thompson, editor of *EZRA--An Online Journal of Translation*, for having found a home for this novel by Tahar Djaout. By having connected me with Bill Lavender of Diálogos, *The Bone Seekers* has, after many years of wandering, reached a safe and sound haven. My warmest thanks goes to both of them.

Last, but never least, there is my profound gratitude to my always meticulous and perceptive first reader, my husband David Vita.

The Bone Seekers

Book I

1

They always managed to arrive at the hottest time of day in the different villages they had to pass through. Crushed by the anvil's scorching heat, cicadas dozed silently on the bark of the ash trees. You could come close to them, hold out your hand and grasp them before they'd even notice. But in the gentle shade of the mosques the people were all there. The solemnity of the moment had banished siesta time everywhere.

Each time someone came by, following right behind a donkey covered with flies, a veteran would put his hand above his eyes like a visor and ask for his identity. Another old man, mechanically fanning himself with a piece of cardboard stuck into a reed, would declare: "That is Saïd Oukaci from the village of Igoudjdal" or "I think that's the son of Ali Madal from the village of Laâzib."

After a few days, however, it became impossible to identify every single person. They were coming from all over—sometimes they were adolescents, barely in their puberty, who didn't even know the set phrases of politeness with which to greet such gatherings. They came by, flushed with embarrassment or heat, arbitrarily hitting their

donkey with their spurs. And sometimes—the height
of sacrilege—they wouldn't even get down off
their animal's back as they crossed the *djemaâ*, the
meeting space. Kids who knew nothing about life yet
were going "to rummage around in the inventories of
death" to wrangle over skeletons the living needed to
assuage the all-too-brazen splash of wealth the new
world was dispensing.

At war's end, the people had organized a frantic
celebration, where endless speeches about fatherland
and fraternity were carelessly manhandled, and
gigantic torches were lit almost everywhere to
prove that the reign of light had been reclaimed, an
undirected generosity that turned each individual's
property into the property of all. Even the rigid
Puritanism, laboriously erected over the centuries,
had exploded. They would all come together at night
in one of the mountain homes with its low doors and
the women would sing in groups of four, spinning
round and round until they dropped.

Then, exhausted from dancing, they stopped for
a moment, staying awake and snorting verbiage,
giving some thought to those who were no longer
there. As if under the force of a sudden order, people
saddled their donkeys and mules, took their pickaxes,
and departed to look for the remains of their dead
and give them a grave worthy of sovereign citizens.
Theirs was an attitude of devotion and self-denial.

The people could very well have raised a barrier between themselves and the past to reinforce their new bliss. They could have thrown out their dead with the putrid bathwater of war to savor in all good conscience a dearly acquired tranquility. But people were attached to their dead as if to an irrefutable proof to be displayed one day before the betrayal of time and man. Donkeys were saddled and the earth would be instructed to bow to the inventory and hand over close to the total number of corpses it had swallowed.

They didn't all leave at the same time but in small waves of two, three or four. Those with the most information left the first day; others had to wait for a final landmark or a vague indication of some small battle before they could equip themselves for the road and the excavations. The war had strewn its victims across a country as wide as the sea. And people would be coming out of their mountain caves and their village communities for the first time to look for their dead in the plains, the pulsating cities, and the vast spaces as bare as a stone. They would discover riches whose abundance and magnificence they had never suspected, unfamiliar objects with strange uses, and people who spoke another language and behaved differently.

The idea of the villagers' self-sacrifice that had circulated will undoubtedly have to be revisited. It was often challenged afterwards. Some individuals even confirmed that the mountain people were on the verge of disowning their dead definitively— despite the watchfulness of one of the leaders of the liberation army who wore a colonial helmet and would carry on all day long about courage and cowardice, the profane and the sacred, the lawful and the forbidden. One fine morning, he had all the villagers assemble in the square and, without any forewarning, cursed them out mercilessly to their parched faces, criticizing their self-centeredness and their propensity to forget, rebuking them for having thought of nothing but their celebratory madness without any consideration for the missing to whom they owed everything.

The terrified villagers didn't have to be told twice. They harnessed their beasts of burden and loaded up on provisions, anticipating the longest of treks. The season was favorable for travel. It was perhaps a little too hot during the day, but the night's gentle balm made a roof and bed unnecessary. When hunger and thirst took over, they could also stop in a field of fig trees or a vineyard and help themselves copiously; the sudden generosity spread out over the land put an end to any formality.

The most despondent were they whose dead had been foolish enough to have fallen very far away. In order to find them, they had to crisscross the entire

country, a plain as long as a relentless summer day,
ever more mountains even harsher than the mountain
at home and more barren than a stony path, only to
end up in a sandy region resembling the unrelenting
Hell that according to the Book is the destiny of the
ungodly. Here there were no trees to provide any
shade, no spring to quench one's thirst, nor figs or
grapes to still one's hunger. Those who returned from
such parts months and months later would describe
places so strange that reasonable people had a hard
time accepting their tales. Blood-red or sandy soil,
heat so fierce that it could cook food, a mind that
might suddenly lose control and go off to cavort
in plains and streams that didn't exist. They would
also talk of the very rare people they had met there,
people whose calm and care were astonishing.

But most of the seekers hadn't gone too far
away. They'd seldom left their mountainous
region, were gone for just a day or two only to
come back triumphantly with a father, a brother or
an acquiescent son whose bones were rattling in a
goatskin or a burlap bag, while their own spirit was
at peace forever.

The cemetery had been laid out in costly fashion
for the remains of these heroes and was so impressive
that many an old man had dreamed ecstatically
of a charitable death that would put him next to
these blissful skeletons. Yes, indeed, the site was

impressive—an entire hillside with a wide vista over the sea had been cleared of its trees and enclosed by a new wire fence. It was the best-placed site in the village; no traveler could miss seeing it. Our dead are the most deserving members of our community, the villagers thought, they alone are worthy of representing us in the eyes of passersby or of those who question us.

The bands of seekers came from different villages, but all who were heading west would travel part of the way together. It was a good road for vehicles, which the occupying forces had created for their tanks and half-tracks. It ran down sharply from a high mountain, charting a network of lines, then flowed on like a stream of quiet water between settlements that lay close together—Idassen, Tabaârourt, Ighil-Mahdi, and Oulmou. At the bend around the last village, the horizon split away from the sea. Shaded by alder and cypress trees, the road descended a little farther, then rushed down in a straight line and ran parallel to the nearby sea whose heaving was very audible now. The next villages— Tifezouine, Agouni, Ouandlous, Abroun—were far less accessible. They could be seen from the road and one wondered how their inhabitants managed to come down and then climb back up again. They were veritable vultures' nests, their red rooftops crowning gigantic, inhospitable rocks. Looking at them, the thought might occur that it would be enough to soar straight down for several hundred yards from way up there and land right in the sea.

The days of summer were at the peak of their force. It seemed the sun had lowered and come a bit closer to earth to rub against the grass and singe it. As soon as dawn broke, the heat announced itself by a vast halo in the east. Then the sky's cauldron began to boil slowly until it reached the bone-white burn that strangled the cicadas' voice and rocked the tall ash trees back and forth. Old men would cling like mollusks to the walls of the mosque searching for a furtive cool buried inside the heart of the stone or roughcast cement. Gandouras left open at the deep neckline showed desiccated bushy torsos. The old men breathed with difficulty like chickens suffocating for lack of air. Surely it would have been more inspiring to remain at home and enjoy a siesta in a cooler place. But people had been chased out of their homes by the occupying army for so long, had seen their horizon shrink so much during the terrible war years, that they preferred to be here, open to the sizzle of the scorching heat, to reclaim all that the war had denied them for so long. With eyes, hands, and lungs wide open, they wanted to recapture the treasured landscapes and feelings of their youth from which they'd been deprived. To bite eagerly into the fluttering blue of the sky, the green coarseness of the trees, the stickiness and warmth of the sap, the mirror of the sinuous rivers, and the searing summer grass.

2

A little cool air would certainly have saved us from the flies. They're worse than the blowtorch of the sky. If only they would disappear under its threat. Real lead pellets boring deliberately into the skin, the real incurable scourge of summer, the horror of beasts of burden and dozing old men. Not only flies, however, persecute the old. There's the irritation caused by overwrought kids, too. Freedom—found once again for some and new to others—had turned the country's customs upside down. Only a few months earlier, for example, nobody would have ever imagined me, fourteen years old next fall, sitting side by side with the old men in the mosque. Their gathering places were strictly prohibited to us. Although I have no idea why, for we'd just realized there's absolutely nothing for us to learn there that we don't already know.

It's simply a matter of the old being embittered and not tolerating us, the young and noisy; it must remind them every minute of the day that death is a pretty sad condition— despite all the rewards and heavenly glories promised to the faithful in the hereafter. We thank you, Almighty God, for letting us be born in the community of the faithful. But even in this time of war when death has become an everyday occurrence that threatens everyone equally, the old men can't be comforted. They know that death, their death, is the saddest and most useless of all. A death that's no more than a formality serves no one, moves no one to pity, a death that has no right to the emphatic words forced daily from the living as they remember someone young that the war cut off in full bloom. A death that will make their own pitiful carcasses into something other than the patriotic remains over which orations burgeon like insatiable maggots. And so, the mosque is all they have left. And they demand to be left in peace there to doze like slumping toads whose coarse and speckled skin is theirs, too.

The new customs of the village have imbued the old men with an unbearable sense of embarrassment. Now the discussions in the mosque always revolve around the young who have fallen on the field of honor, while they, old men, try hard to curl into themselves like spineless, repugnant individuals having the effrontery of being alive when so many vigorous, deserving youth have been sleeping beneath the earth for years. Those whose son or grandson was killed by bullets are even more guilt-ridden—cowards, egoists, unworthy sires that they are, could they themselves not have gone off to face death first, as nature requires? Hypocritical custodians of a wisdom they don't even respect, aren't they supposed to remember that those who come first should be the first to depart?

Still, there are some old men I really like a lot, who don't in any way deserve the plight of beaten and consenting dog that has become theirs. For instance, there is Hand Ouzerouk, a spindly man with a ruddy face who tells very funny off-color stories to the young while he glances around to make sure his peers aren't listening. Before the war, he had a stall by the road close to the village where he used to sell all kinds of things, especially fabrics for women.

These days, when the old men are together in the mosque they're completely flustered, for they don't know what to talk about. Their discussions about the everlasting topics of life—heat, night, water, fruit, harvests—are quickly done. At times they're overjoyed when they find a reason to curse the flies or when they notice an increase in the temperature worthy of commentary. But then the oppressive victory of silence reigns again. I see the old men with their nodding heads having great difficulty breathing, toads on the verge of passing over into the hereafter of repulsive animals. Is there no humanity left then among people? Is there no feeling of compassion anymore that would make someone take the hand of one of these dethroned elders and flood him with kind and comforting words that would help him understand he still has a legitimate place here on earth?

No, Hand Ouzerouk, he does not accept the well-founded predicament reserved for the old. He rails against anyone he chooses, stands up to any of the armed and glorious men who impress everyone else, talks about women and certain forbidden topics with a freedom barely conceivable in this village of straightforward mores where people don't even dare sneeze unless it's in the approved fashion.

Rabah Ouali, his companion, is a good deal younger than he but also more complex. Every now and then he laughs at people who think they're terribly important, but he knows how to be conciliatory, even timorous when things turn sour. His language is less brash and abrasive than Hand Ouzerouk's, but I like his anecdotes and his strange way of turning a serious discussion around at will.

When they told me I was to leave with Rabah Ouali I was not unhappy at all. I would, of course, have preferred Hand Ouzerouk as a companion for a long journey, but adults sometimes make incomprehensible choices.

I didn't know that I, too, was supposed to go. Having repeatedly watched the anachronistic convoys in which men and animals, covered with the same transforming layer of dust and under the same hellish heat, all looked alike, I never would have guessed that I myself would one day be among these cheerful exhumers.

My brother, who had died on the battlefield three years before, is therefore one of these piles of bones as well. I thought my mother and my disabled father had more tenderness and consideration for him. In some more delicate nook of these jagged mountain layers, I thought true love would exist, able to withstand the exhibitionist and predatory madness that had suddenly goaded human beings with respect toward those they had sometimes loved the most. But here it was, every family and every person needed their very own little handful of bones to justify the arrogance and important bearing that would characterize their future behavior on the village square. The bones form a rather comical prelude to the profusion of papers, certificates, and other substantiation that a short time later would render their appearance and law implacable. Woe to him who won't have any bones or documentation to show when faced with the disbelief of his peers! Woe to him who won't have understood that words have become worthless and that the era of oral pledges is gone forever!

Since we have no horse, Ali Amaouche agreed to let us borrow his mount. I don't know what miracle occurred, however, because usually he is more attached to his donkeys than his children. But these

times of euphoria and blissful lunacy have changed
so many people's attitudes and feelings! In any
event, Amaouche's pride in his donkeys is perfectly
well-founded; he has always had the most beautiful
animals in the village—with well-cropped manes
and tails, rubbed down and lustrous coat, always
new and clattering shoes. The very names he gives
his donkeys show a great deal of affection—Tikouk,
Bouriche or Mhand nath Mhand, depending on their
size, hide, and speed.

"Arrrgh," he's in the habit of yelling as he leads
his donkeys through the steep alleys, "May God
change you into a horse!" No one in the village would
have had the gall to buy a donkey or a mule without
first asking for Ali Amaouche's invaluable advice.

And so he agreed to lend us his beast, but he
followed him home with us, worried, checking on
the packsaddle and the shoes, having a last quick
look at his collar and chest, and bombarding us
with suggestions, recommendations, and pleas. Real
concerns a mother might have about a spoiled or
grumpy child. We had to provide endless reassurances
and come up with a whole set of promises.

The mystery of my being accompanied by Rabah
Ouali will soon be cleared up. I was to learn that in
some vague way we were blood relatives and my
parents were undoubtedly eager to make the most
of that sense of indestructible solidarity that blood

weaves among mountain people, before it, too,
would disappear as had so many traditions that once
were thought to be ineradicable.

Ali Amaouche stayed there to supervise us
through the final preparations. He was afraid we'd
load his donkey down too much. So we had to make
do with scant gear and just a few provisions—two
pickaxes, one shovel, one burlap bag, two satchels
with some biscuits and dried figs, and a calabash
with whey. Still, Ali Amaouche was worried; one last
piece of advice—not to use his donkey too much for
riding; but he knew this was a pointless suggestion.

Usually, when mountain people have to travel
they get up at dawn to cover some distance before
it gets too hot. But the new conditions in the country
have altered even the most ingrained habits and the
most natural actions. There's a feeling that people
have suddenly discovered the luxurious satisfaction
of disregarding what is customary and prohibited.
One after the other, all barriers have taken wing
with a speed and vehemence that only a few years
earlier would have been impossible to imagine, often
surprising even the staunchest dissenters.

When we left the village to go west, the sun had
gone down quite a bit in the sky's immaculate arc.
Rabah Ouali was walking right beside the donkey.

I followed a few steps behind him. I had no idea where I was going but was glad to leave the village—for how long?—, the harsh setting of my wretched childhood.

3

Summer has congealed gesture and sound. The sun's heavy white silence moves the hours forward without help. As we travel I discover that this Rabah Ouali is unimaginably different from the one I got to know in the village. That damned village with its invisible but rigid obstructions rising suddenly, threateningly, before the first careless individual who dares to hold his spoon with his left hand. With its moronic restrictions and hypocrisy that shape the cornerstone of its communal life. I wonder how people keep going, putting on a lifelong act without exploding—as Hand Ouzerouk often does—in bright daylight, showing their true feelings, moods, and indignation. And then, the height of mockery, even they who went to die elsewhere beneath more temperate skies facing the sea or in the tranquil immensity of stony deserts or rocky plateaus, even their remains and memory are now brought back to this tyrannical village. This village that throughout their lives had inhibited their breathing freely, stretching their limbs in the full benevolent sun, even if that sun squeezes bodies until their most concealed secretions come spurting out. The best thing I can hope for is that my brother's bones will not be found, which are buried somewhere in soil more hospitable than the parcel of land whose mores and inflexibility are molded in the image of its rocks.

My brother can only be comfortable where he now rests. At any rate, it would be impossible for him to feel worse there than here at home. I remember him very well. A rather gangly shepherd whose life wasn't very pleasant. His only pride lay in our dog Boobit and a Basque beret that he sported with great ostentation. Especially my father made his life very difficult. His entire universe consisted of sheep, goats, reed flutes, and rabbit snares. He'd always dreamed of going on a walking expedition to the nearest city, but he never managed to bring this to fruition before he picked up the rifle that would overturn the draconian laws in control of his life.

Even today, when I happen to think of my brother, I see a huge stone covered with white lichen. This stone sits in Bouharoun, a field we own not far from the village. It's there and at the house that I mostly saw my brother. I'd always find him sitting on the huge rock, daydreaming or playing the flute. Our maternal uncle—who would also die in the war— had one day given him a lovely metal flute he had decorated by using a knife. It was the happiest day of my brother's life.

A model shepherd he was not, far from it. Had

our father been able to do so, he would have rolled that reprehensible stone, witness to all my brother's distractions and other forms of apathy, all the way to hell. I wonder what kind of a peasant my brother would have made had he lived beyond the age of a shepherd boy. It's a question with depressing prospects, one my father must have asked himself repeatedly.

Fortunately, one fine day my brother realized it all. He'd come home, unrecognizable, filled with a strength and with certainties that stunned my parents. He left at night and we didn't see him again for two years; then when he returned, also at night, he was even less recognizable. He'd grown taller, more striking, authoritarian and cheerful, even with his emaciated face. His military uniform and his submachine gun (he told us it was made in China) didn't encumber him at all. Such bearing, such presence! And how he impressed my father. Gone was the gawky shepherd clutching his huge lichen-covered rock like a slug! He had a handsome young man with him, blond like one of the soldiers of the occupation, who spoke our language with a funny accent.

I don't know where my mother managed to find so many good things to eat, we knew nothing about their presence under our roof—white couscous with eggs and bits of fat, delicious dried meat, and honey cakes.

My brother had done away with his previous dark temperament. He ate and joked and was brimming with witticisms. He entertained us with stories about places and villages he'd passed through (such a compensation, such overindulgence for one who used to dream of simply going to the next village and then never did!). He was using new words whose meaning I didn't know. As I listened to him, I decided he'd turned out to be an important person, was living in a secret kingdom (a kind of aerial place that can't be seen during the day but is all lit up at night, full of fantastic movement) where men were big brothers, courageous and protective.

How sweet it was to imagine my brother expanding in this fabulous and chivalrous world, having escaped from the oppressive daily routine that was ours under the knell of the occupying soldiers. I knew his was an intransigent world but a fair one, where one acquired everlasting respectability. He who went into the army—whatever his original social status—would take on an aura of incomparable prestige in the eyes of the villagers. When they talked about these folks (which they did only furtively) they used special terms used just on extraordinary occasions, terms that gave you gooseflesh and compelled respectful silence— the land, honor, God, blood, and brotherhood. My brother was as handsome as he was imposing; his slenderness and his gaunt face were no reminder of the sickly adolescent of previous years. They merely increased his elegance.

And here we are today, on our way to find his presumed skeleton. In one unforeseeable and dazzling leap he'd left the wretchedness that torments children and their crazy dreams. But did he know that this same leap would propel him into the world beyond? How had he, the shepherd who'd never been especially lively or daring, welcomed death? They say that the young peasants who joined the resistance died with exemplary courage. Sublime young men, or pitiable youth? Now they lie beneath the immovable stone, now they're past breathing or trembling, they who didn't even have time to learn what life can offer to the mind and body of the young in laughter and emotions.

Gentle familiarity of death; death as cyclical and fatal as wheat, as bitter laurel and sweet grape. Now they are growing into songs on the lips of women and into eloquent words in the gatherings of men, they whom death mowed down under fire in the firmness of their flesh.

The mountain's name is Tamgout, a synonym of certain death but also of immaculate snow, of freedom in the heights' virginal air. The women are beautiful and desirable despite the circles under their eyes and the wartime rags they wear. Their belly is the cruel vessel of life and death, holding hands in the absolute. The triumph of firm and vulnerable flesh! The women have tamed death with their calm beauty, and their wild, raw-boned jackal cries ring out in the face of the terrorized occupier. They accompany us in the search for skeletons and sing to defuse anguish and paralyzing fear. They sing to eliminate the bitterness from their tears.

Mountain, lay flat your peaks
so we can see the places of our childhood.
Mountain, be merciful
to the boys who lie among your stones.

But Tamgout is unperturbed. Like the harvesting scythe of death in motion. Tamgout is sheltering and murderous. The face suddenly inverted, incomprehensible, like a mother cat devouring its young. Every time I thought of all these dead, I saw the oxen attached two by two, turning doggedly in the summer's overheated atmosphere. And I saw the color yellow, too. The color of heatwaves and wheat dust. The color of high-flying dreams where clouds of grain devour heedless insects. In the past, when I was just beginning to discover the enchantment of the fields of summer, my brother and I had made a bet on death.

It was a scorching hot day like today. In the

distance where it joined the sky, the sea was a
motionless blue line. I went to look for my brother
on his huge stone covered with sun-roasted mold.
The ruminating goats were lying in the shade of
an olive tree and the sheep were huddled together,
panting, subdued, like dogs led astray on a wrong
path. Suddenly a scratchy sound in the foraged grass.
We looked up at the same time. A little lizard, the
color of early springtime grass, was walking slowly
toward the stone. I said to my brother:

"Who created the little lizard?"

"The big lizard."

"And who created the big lizard?"

"The shimmering lizard."

"And who created the shimmering lizard?"

"The marsh crocodile."

"And who created the marsh crocodile?"

"Your mother's Good Lord."

"Can the lizard die?"

"Of course," he answered, "I'll bet you a basket
of grapes for two olive pits."

And, taking his wooden staff, he dealt the lizard
such a blow that its tail came off. But instead of dying
under our very eyes, the little reptile's two sections
quivered for a moment and then vanished in opposite
directions.

It was a scorching hot day like today. And death
was slyly wandering around between the stalks of

youth. Death in labor birthing glory and songs that
were breaking in the throats of beautiful women.
Death once used to signify old men subjugated by
decay, with gangrenous and oozing limbs; they were
sick, some sort of epidemic festering inside them,
while the people closest to them would finally grow
weary and disgusted. Then one day death took on the
face of vigor and youthful grace, the face of eternal
youth suddenly struck down in full flight. Women
painted their eyes blue so they could weep more
elegantly, they drank honey early in the morning to
smooth the warm, impassioned modulations of their
voice.

Mountain, lay flat your peaks
so we can see the places of our childhood.
Mountain, be merciful
to the boys who lie among your stones.

Rabah Ouali is far from being endowed with a
hero's good looks. His nose resembles a sweet potato
and his corpulence makes him look like a bear on
a leash. His chances are pretty slim of someday
supplying the women's songs with any material that
extols physical beauty and masculine excellence.
Even slimmer are his chances of being cut down in
full bloom by that wartime death that lays the young
in glory-spangled shrouds. Unbearable summers,

blackish manure spread across the autumn fields, flies, donkeys, and predictable things concerning sun and rain—that is the stranglehold universe from which Rabah Ouali can never escape. So he has opted to just kid around. To take revenge on the injustice of destiny that makes some handsome and others too ordinary, some heroic and others nameless. Maybe he carries some aggression in his heart, some secret wounds may lie hidden in the undisclosed recesses of memory. It's very hard to know. His love of living at any cost is too strong to let him make a breach in the blockhouse of his caution. Villagers are cruel; when they detect a crack in the wall that obscures each person's life, the latter is forever lost. Rabah Ouali is on his guard, ready with his irony to rebuff any attempt at penetrating his pathetic existence. He never loses his temper, for fear of surrendering his perfect self-control if only for a moment and allowing his shell to open. Never angry at anything or anyone. Not even at fate's disparaging blows. To justify his ill-placed calm whenever it looks as if things are starting to go badly, Rabah Ouali pronounces a curative formula whose very modern elements escape most of the villagers: "Take your foot off the brake of life and let the planet orbit where it will."

4

The sun attached itself to a point on my forehead and has begun to bore in. My memory is lava slush in which grasshoppers cavort with a pile of scorched leaves that have been crumpled under the feet of people walking by. Everything around us has begun to live intensely as if its presence and weight were being felt for the very first time. The sun deals its crushing blows, the air quavers like a liquid surface, and the hills fend us off with invisible but powerful hands.

Villages, your squares that are now like cauldrons are so unwelcoming to worn-out feet and shoulders! The sleepy looks intruding on our peregrinations and our stops hardly inspire us to stay and ask for even just a sip of water! The pitiless summer has set man's generosity aflame and the villages we pass through are no more than a desert hidden under red rooftops. In the past I yearned to see as many villages as possible, I thought that every one of them would have new things to show. And when some boy I knew would return from this or that town, I felt consumed by jealousy. But I'm beginning to realize these feelings were unfounded. Nothing resembles any village more than the next one. Ighil-Mahdi, Tifezouine, Taïncert, Azaghar, the only thing each hamlet has to offer your curiosity is the same tiny square, the same bare trees, the same unbearable heat, and the same summer's widespread drowsiness. Only those villages that have a view over the open sea invite you to stay a moment and inhale deeply.

The first pleasant surprise is our arrival in Anezrou, the large town my brother had so much wanted to visit in his crazy shepherd's dreams. Living here must be equal to having a vast choice of delights. Not all the colonials have left yet; some of them, mostly older men, walk their leashed dogs in a restricted park with scrubbed green benches; a stream of water urinates continually up into the air. With their inoffensive, scared or pathetic looks the colonists are mystifying. All the foreigners we saw in our village were brutal military men; but there really do seem to be some civilians like ourselves among them. Travel can teach you such incredible things!

We made our first stop in Anezrou. At the entrance stood a clump of eucalyptus trees to which the rural people tie their donkeys. Then a lovely wide boulevard runs through the town from one end to the other. There's a dizzying bustle and the traffic of people is intense. Shops of all kinds offer their wares to the passersby. How happy I would have been if I'd had some relatives in this city so I could spend a few

days eating and drinking the delicious things that we
don't find in the village.

Jostled and solicited, we wandered around among
the crowd. The foodstuffs in the shop windows rushed
at our nose and stomach. I wondered if my guide and
companion was going to have us taste a delicious bit
of some unfamiliar cake. But that would be counting
too much on the favorable gestures of adults. Rabah
Ouali had certainly told me a few funny anecdotes,
but banter doesn't satisfy the stomach. A little lost,
we're going here and there through the wide city
streets. They're totally straight and jammed with
parked cars. Rabah Ouali knows many of these
vehicles' names.

The boys I come across only increase my
bitterness—their faces breathe good health, their
clothes are clean, and all of them look as if in their
life there's no place whatsoever for lice, shame,
obstacles, dung, and the rural tasks of gathering
and weeding. Those who speak our language do so
with tactful affectation; others handle the colonial
language comfortably and well.

I was unaware that God was this unfair. But in
the village they never stop repeating that we come
from honorable backgrounds, that we belong to
respectable families, and that we should constantly
be on our guard for fear of ruining our reputation
and our prestige. Oh, to be like these boys from

the fountain "pissing toward heaven', just to live in cleanliness, warmth, and gentle luxury like them— and, why not?—, just to own one of those longed-for toys, a camera, a little radio. For that, I would have sacrificed not only the dubious privilege as the family son but also every tie with the village. Besides, others have done exactly that. Countless others, in fact. Out of some sense of decency or caution no one mentions their names in conversation. Now I understand them, these sons of very pious, very respectable, and very poor families, who cross the sea once and say farewell to their past. Despite a superficial indifference, the villagers rush out each time to see the ones who come back, for a few years running they inquire after prodigal sons or fathers, then out of pessimism and a sense of decorum, the relatives seal off their hearts and respond to fate with stony silence. They are called "lost and astray" for all time and are, indeed, seen as such.

I don't know whether our itinerary has more enjoyable places in store for us. But it's not very likely. Even the sea here seems particularly tame and welcoming with its dikes and carefully fitted ramparts. The city itself is too clean. There's no place for dung, for braying, for the acquiescent walk of donkeys that must stay in the thicket of eucalyptus at the entrance to inhale the sea wind and watch the cars go by.

We meet people from our own and neighboring villages. They all seem both busy and roughed up by this world that eludes them. They barely take the time to greet you, then they're off again, swallowed up in a whirlwind of inextricable things. People have discovered they can now become rich and respected, that they can possess invaluable goods without opening a wallet. The word has spread—from here on in, the country has a government that belongs to all people and has wealth to be distributed by the handful. Therefore, many villagers have abandoned their homes and, to be less encumbered, have sold their two oxen and their paltry herd of goats or sheep. They lined up in front of the local administration building waiting for manna, sometimes spending the night there so as not to miss the first minute the doors open.

They've replaced the honor code and the ancestral customs with another code, comprised of papers, abstracts of registration documents, various certificates, and cards in different colors. Folders began to grow fat with paperwork and the peasants had to appeal continuously to literate people to help them tell one document from another.

Unfortunately, we stayed in Anezrou just long enough to let the donkey rest and breathe the sea air, while allowing Rabah Ouali a little time to rummage around in the bureaucratic dealings to see whether there was any way for him to intercept a small—and highly unlikely—windfall but then, in these times that defy all understanding, who is to know?

We certainly aren't getting any taste of the gastronomic delicacies of the little town. We continue our trek across desolate fields, almost impassable trails, and past villages balancing precariously on top of high peaks. When night begins to fall, we light a fire between some stones and do our cooking.

5

"Da Rabah, those papers every citizen is chasing after so eagerly, what are they good for, anyway?"

"The future, my boy, is an enormous stationery store where every notebook and every folder will be worth its weight in gold a hundred times over. Woe unto those who don't show up in the correct register!"

"Do you, too, have a right to some of these cards and certificates?"

"Yes, my friend, but the cards come in different colors referring to the color of specific events. I was in the war but in a strange sort of way, and I had some pretty difficult times with the occupying army."

"And yet, you spent the entire war in the village."

"Sure, I did, but appearances aren't everything. Surely you remember the time when the army held the whole village under police custody, when all of us were starving, when people didn't have enough food for just one meal a day. Even acorns, grass, carobs—the last resort for fighting famine—became impossible to find. Every night four of us would go out with our donkeys, trying to collect whatever we could in the nearby fields to keep our wretched life going. For a while we were luckier than the rest of the villagers, although we always helped them with a handful of fruit or a bunch of edible grass. After all, a good Muslim can't very well stuff himself with all sorts of meadow plants until his lips and gums turn green like young apples, while his neighbor is chewing on the springtime wind. Then one ill-fated night a patrol surprised us in the fields. Warnings. Bursts of fire. Screams. Fortunately, none of us was hit. We were caught, shoved, beaten, and taken back to the camp with our donkeys. There we were ordered to admit that the purpose of our nocturnal escapade was to connect with the underground and provide them with food. Atrocities. Assaults. Bruises. They threw us in a cellar where we stayed for three days. When it was formally established that our nightly excursions had nothing to do with the underground, they set us free. But the experience in the cell had been so decisive that not one of us dared to risk another foray. So we had to put up with adding more notches to our belts, which already had plenty of them as it was.

"One day, however, hunger forced us to make a new plan and we started our excursions again. Once by the light of the moon, while we were digging through the military dump that would sometimes contain cans of sardines—a bit damaged but still delicious—, I discovered an envelope that for some incomprehensible reason I immediately slipped into my pocket. Maybe I expected to find money. I can't remember. When I came home, I had my son Chaâbane read the letter to me. I found out that the epistle was addressed to Jean-Pierre Leloup, the lieutenant commander of the camp, and that it came from his father. The letter surprised me very much because I didn't know there were foreigners who thought about us that way. The father was reminding his son that he came from a highly respectable family and that under no circumstances was he to be cruel toward the people whose country he happened to be occupying. In the letter he also mentioned factory work, disagreements, and struggles the significance of which I didn't really understand. I suppose Lieutenant Leloup didn't take the advice very seriously since the letter had ended up in a garbage dump. As for me, little did I suspect that my curiosity would one day save my life.

"My comrades in misfortune and I were again caught by a patrol and taken to the camp, where they separated us. Each of us was now presented with a punishment compared to which our first imprisonment seemed like a motherly reprimand. Lieutenant Leloup had come to witness the torture sessions for himself. Seeing him enter the hole where my torturers had tied me up, I frantically called out to him:

"'Lieutenant Leloup, you come from a highly

respectable family and your father would never have stood for seeing you act this way.'

"He didn't seem to understand immediately. He wasn't even sure that it was I who had spoken. What did his family have to do with this hellhole, anyway? But he had to face the facts and approached me.

"'You know my father?'

"'Do I know your father? Louis Leloup, resident of Mons-en-Puelle in the north. That's where I spent all my time before the war when I was working in France. We even worked in the same factory for a while.'

"At first the officer remained speechless, then:

"'Why didn't you ever tell me this?'

"'Because I don't want to bother you with the sad stories of my life. The law is the law, and I've never wanted anyone to do me any favors.'

"Then, addressing himself to my miserable tormentors, he ordered:

"'Set him free at once.'

"From then on, they stopped hassling me about my nightly excursions, which soon no longer served only to gather acorns, carob, and edible grass, but essentially to establish connections with the brothers in the underground."

These days, the night falls later and later, as it wanders around the folds in the mountains before settling down heavily over the earth. All the exhaustion accumulated in my body surfaces, tethering my limbs and weighing down on my eyelids. But Rabah Ouali thinks we should first get closer to the sea. The temperature there, he says, is gentler at night. His voice reaches me, weaving itself laboriously across miles of air thick as cotton batting.

6

The sun rose early, its rays waltzing across the sea. Splendid dawns that fix the shattered body and harness the will to move on toward other horizons, go on other treks. What a fine memory you need to squeeze in so many colors entangled side by side, so many virginal muggy smells, so many infinitesimal suspended cries interweaving in the air like a spiderweb letting beams of light pass through. The ground under our feet is hard, but the hills glimpsed in the distance waver, overtaken by light as if by an endless vertigo. Our stops have become regulated— the first one around eleven o'clock, another one at four, and finally one for the night.

My appetite is insatiable now; several times a day I feel like begging Rabah Ouali to stop so we can take a handful of dried figs from our bags or to pinch some enticing fruit from the orchards by the side of the road. But I know that we must walk, for ours is a solemn mission that is intolerant of weakness. What does an insidious stomach cramp matter next to these bones we seek, bones of a martyr whose happy master is gamboling in the celestial gardens? That's the greatest advantage for men who've perished in battle. More than the transient songs of women who keep singing them for only a few years, more than the costly plaques in the cemeteries, more than the registers where their names are inscribed, the most valuable reward is the one they enjoy in the hereafter. All of them. Without any exception. When God takes it upon himself to reward his faithful he does so most extravagantly.

"Da Rabah, what is that Paradise where the martyrs dwell?"

"Paradise, my boy, has immense thoroughfares, gleaming with magnificence and purity. Its sidewalks are littered with gigantic honey-soaked crepes. Apple trees sag under the weight of their fruit; a single apple is so big it needs two hands to be held. Watermelons bursting open from the pressure of their juice that flows like a brook beneath your feet. The partridges of Paradise? They're as large as turkeys here on earth. One gesture—what am I saying?—just the thought alone, and there's poultry cooked in the sauce of your choice. But most impressive of all are the two parallel rivers, one all butter, the other all honey, which will never run dry, no matter how hot the summer or how often they're dipped into."

Da Rabah's Paradise made me even hungrier. It's a paradise made to measure for those whose empty insides incessantly growl. I hope that from here on in there's a seat reserved for me up there.

"And the Good Lord is so generous that he lets the many men who've fallen in battle luxuriate in Paradise?"

"Nothing can wear down or undermine the Good Lord's indulgence. His heart is as wide as the full breadth of the continents. His appearance is equally impressive. He is a true grandfather with a beard many miles long, which he sometimes leaves trailing in the heavens like an immaculate cloud. He has no ascendants or descendants, he's without age and without hate. And what makes him prevail on the throne of the Universe is his great patience and his ability to forgive the most sinful of actions. As you know, each one of us has two angels that accompany us everywhere, and each one of them has a ledger; the angel on your right shoulder keeps track of your good actions, the one on your left shoulder notes down your transgressions. God calls them together periodically to hear their official depositions. But the angel of good is always the first to speak. Without any notebook or pen, God can keep it all in his head—nodding from time to time, and when an exceptionally fine action is mentioned he smiles a little. When it's the second angel's turn, the old man is already tired. He listens with half an ear, or not at all, and sometimes dozes off, which means that he lets man get away with quite a few of his nasty tricks."

Rabah Ouali is not always talkative, but when his energy is unleashed and he becomes garrulous, the hours and miles pass at an incredible speed. The first stop, at eleven, comes upon us just like that although my legs were expecting to continue for many more interminable miles.

Sometimes we run into other groups who, like ourselves, are looking for skeletons. Some are large, others consist simply of one man and his animal. We walk part of the way together and talk mostly of the abomination of the recent past, of the relentless war that spared neither young nor old and ensnared many animals on its list of murderous achievements, too. "Even dogs and donkeys weren't able to escape from their savagery", our chance companions would invariably repeat. Then we'd separate in the overwhelming heat that slices the air with swift strokes, blurring the road before us.

But since the sea has been our companion, the heat wave seems almost dissolved, swallowed up by that huge blue belly. A gentle breeze touches our face, bringing an invading composite scent that fuses tree saps, the decay of the undergrowth, a multitude of sea creatures, a taste of departure without return.

The breeze invites us to walk on forever. And that's what I truly would have liked to do. To walk just to be walking, with the sound of the waves by my side, before me an endless dawn, white as the foam when it's angry. Without any prospect of a skeleton or a return to the village when we reach our final stopping point. For the thought of my brother's skeleton weighs upon my back like a load of thorns. What will it be like when we really have him with us, that silent but exasperating companion? Often, I try to forget him. I do my utmost to convince myself we're making our way toward some city or some long-forgotten relative. But every time a splinter of my painful burden inserts itself to call me to order, reminding me unceremoniously of our sad vulture-like goal.

Why is everyone so eager to unearth these glorious dead and change the site of their graves at all costs? Perhaps they want to be reassured that they're really dead and will never come back to demand their share of the celebration, to contest our speeches and patriotic demonstrations, our happiness as escapees from an otherwise blind and merciless war. Or perhaps, they quite simply value their being interred more deeply in the earth than all the other dead. Just try to figure people out! They mourn those who, they claim, in the whole world are most dear to them and then rush off to exhume their remains, only to bury them more hermetically.

The cicadas never fail to keep us company. Their singing begins early in the morning and gets louder as the heat rises, their song as heavy as a tombstone. When we make our afternoon stop at four, the volume slowly starts to decrease. Then other insects and animals gradually usurp the cooling air. Grasshoppers, crickets, lizards, and geckos enter the night with their quavering cries. Cries of praise to darkness and the god of viscosity, cries of spirited and impatient love, cries of apprehension or fear, cries of savage joy on the body of captured prey.

Night is even more intensely alive than day. Its skin rises and bristles under the unsettling lips of the breeze. Odors sweet or acrid are set free in undulating waves. Like a conquered dominated female no longer in control of her secretions. In the beginning I was frightened of spending the night outside. I would continually turn around, hold my breath, frozen with fear at the least little swishing in the grass. But in the end I got used to it. I discovered that the night actually doesn't hide any enemies and that, on the contrary, the many discreet breathing sounds or other noises are often the expression of well-intentioned vigilance, a kind of regular reminder indicating everything's for the best, that any potential danger will be neutralized. And so, I learned to sleep in the embracing familiarity of all those little lives that beat feverishly while waiting for the sun to calm them down and allow them, in turn, to sleep. I let myself be rocked by the plaintive sounds of love, the hidden buzzing and, with the help of my fatigue, my eyes close very quickly and I sleep straight through.

The most beautiful sounds are those of the busy dawn. Gelling fragments vibrating in the sky. And then the magic of the early morning birds! I can distinguish every intermingled song. Lark, warbler, blackbird or redstart. The voice that's fascinating, though, is the heartrending wail of the blue roller as it rises and descends. It dies down in endless sadness and then surges once again.

Comforting companions on our grimy route, you have lifted our treks with such sky-blue notes and elegance! I have a very long history with feathered animals. Nests I discovered with eggs inside, followed by the triumphant ascent of life, from the blind little bits of flesh fluttering and squeaking to the elegant young singing bird trying out its uncertain wings. I've held so many birds in my smug, sometimes destructive hands. Warm or trembling feathers with the forge of the heart pulsing underneath.

Other birds are always following us. Doleful birds of prey high in the sky where they keep a careful watch, their enlarged shadows forming huge stains on the ground below. Our most constant companions. Perhaps they understand that our mutual plans conceal an obvious similarity.

7

*F*ood is the favorite, inexhaustible topic of conversation of this country's population.

Ever since we've become independent and can eat our fill, the behavior of many has unexpectedly and mysteriously changed. They've stopped visiting each other, stopped lending each other small kitchen implements—and at the same time they've abandoned the custom of shrouding their actions and property in deepest secrecy. Before, traditions of honor and good neighborliness required that any rare staple (meat, fruit) be shared with close family members or neighbors, or else be taken home but only with great precaution so no one could possibly discover any sign of its presence. Now, in contrast, there's arrogance and provocation. It's all about who can pile the greatest amount of waste in front of his door and who can hang the largest number of expensive and tempting items in his window. Now people own goods and things they couldn't even dream of before—shiny straight-angled devices used to make music, to keep cold, to bring heat, bright light, soft light, wind, stable and precarious balance, fixed or moving images.

But food continues to be the big deal. Until now, its previously unknown variety had been surprising and disorienting, posing endless problems. Can you really eat three courses at one sitting? But which one do you start with? And if you fill yourself up with the first one how do you handle the next two? Even within the family this sudden, excessive abundance gave rise to hilarious conflicts. The usual triggers are the old toothless mothers-in-law—who say to themselves: "Now that we have nothing with which to chew anymore, the unfair God floods us with good things"—who can't bear to see their daughters-in-law eat their fill. It seems absurd to them, an unprecedented affront. Were they deprived during their youth, deprived even of dried figs and the blackish rye couscous that scours your throat, only so that in their old age they'd be watching lazy shameless young women stuff themselves like prized cattle? Now that they'd lost both teeth and appetite, life still kept turning its back on God's creatures. No, the times were too unfair, too unrewarding. With their sharp sense of punishment and proper perspective, wouldn't the guardian saints vanish, overcome by the insult of the opulence and magnificence of these new times?

On the road like us also looking for his brother's bones, and truly obsessed with his stomach, it's

Chérif Oumeziane who tells us the news that there will be an important sacrifice tomorrow in a place known as La-Source-de-la-Vache. All morning long a microphone inside the minaret of the mosque in Anezrou had been making the announcement. He himself had to go farther south but it was important to him to make this detour before continuing his journey—for strictly pious reasons, he made sure to tell us. He started giving us long explanations about the holy site, the sacred remains that rested there, and about the no less saintly chosen one who today prudently looks after all these spiritual goods. Neither Rabah Ouali nor I interrupted him, for he's deafer than a tree stump, and when anyone in his presence so much as moves his lips he grows so confused and tense, makes such persistent and painful efforts to understand, that people who know him well have decided to remain absolutely silent when they're with him.

"Meat has become a common food today. And the way to prepare it has also changed, you know. You don't just let it simmer in a sauce full of chickpeas anymore! They've discovered all sorts of fine-smelling combinations, one more mysterious than the next. If I described some of them to you, you'd double up and never stop laughing. There's a whole multitude of herbs, oils, vegetables, and even sweet things that go into these strange sauces.

Yes, obviously it's not the end of the world, because somewhere they still make you those dense couscous dishes in which you can make nice rivulets to pour olive oil in.

"Seven grown oxen will be waiting for the pilgrims tomorrow. Yes, just give us that lovely solid fat meat from which the juices flow like melted butter when you bite into it. I've seen it before. But then I was only watching. There were three powerful men whose thick beards made them look like patriarchs. They had a little donkey with a bulging belly, stooped beneath a mysterious load carefully concealed under some dirty blankets. They were each wrapped in a wide faded burnoose despite the season, which was either springtime or summer, as far as I recall. Each of their hoods was pulled backwards by the weight of a holy book with rigid corners, an inkwell, and a bunch of pens made of reeds, trimmed and sharpened at the ends. The color of their clothes gave the impression that these men had spent their entire lives in front of a fireplace while a rain of soot was coming down on them."

The three travelers were very talkative, constantly interspersing their sentences with words in a language I didn't understand. The villagers soon surrounded them, looking very humble, like pupils dutifully listening to a distinguished master. Repeatedly, the three men took the inkwells from their hoods and scribbled mysterious, illegible prescriptions on yellowish graph paper. I soon realized that they knew the secrets of life, knew the reason for every fact and every thing, and could cure all kinds of illnesses, both visible and hidden.

They didn't even have to indicate they were hungry. As soon as the sun reached its zenith, a goat was slaughtered, carved, and prepared in a lentil sauce. I think it was Ferhat Akli, the most destitute and without question also the most devout man in the village, who had agreed to this expenditure. Only the innards and the offal were taken out and given to the cooks and the children of the family. Even the head and the four legs had been taken to the meeting place where the three strangers, whom I began to hate with dark but profound intensity, had lost their verbosity, waiting in nervous silence. Tense to the breaking point, the attention was totally focused on the dish of couscous and the goat, which were slow to reach their carnivorous jaws. When the large bowl was placed before them they began to protest, only as a matter of form, but the claws on their predatory fingers had already hooked big pieces of meat.

Silently we watched them eat. All you heard was the insidious noise of clenched chewing. After a few minutes, a feeling of untenable indecency began to float over it all, and the adults intervened to chase us away. Ashamed and disgusted the children dispersed, without even trying to protest as they always did when they were being denied a spectacle they felt they had a right to enjoy. But I found a little hiding place behind a cracked wall and started spying on the strangers.

They ate without speaking, almost without looking at each other. The only thing that came out of their mouth between chunks of meat and couscous were sighs and grunts. Sweat dribbled down their foreheads onto their eyes. Every now and then the men would stop eating, wipe their greasy hands on their already filthy burnoose, and take a gulp of cool water.

The arduous struggle with the food lasted a good half hour and then, after very loudly uttering a formula to glorify their generous God in thanks for the meat dishes, the three warriors put down their spoons at the same time and wiped their hands on their bushy beards. They kept them there for a moment while they mumbled blessings to the devout and charitable person who had so royally regaled the wanderers whose love of the sacred word had driven them onto the road.

The image of this astounding meal haunted me for several days. I'd just given a hefty shape and a face to the ogres in the folk tales. And even today, every time I'm present at some grotesque indulgence of food, I think of these monsters hiding beneath

their revolting burnooses. I used to enjoy imagining
them devouring their donkey on the way, right after
they left our village. Besides, ogres like that haven't
completely disappeared; of course, they wash and
perfume their beards, they wear whiter and finer
burnooses. But I'm sure that tomorrow you'll find
a dozen or so of them around the dishes that will
circulate among the pilgrims at the sacrifice of La-
Source-de-la-Vache.

8

The protective saint—Sidi Maâchou ben Bouziane, may his name be praised until the end of time— grants only one wish at a time. Poor wretches ask for a good crop of fava beans or oats on their parcels of unproductive land; sterile couples beg for a male child. One has to believe that miracles unfailingly occur, for not a single week goes by without a pilgrim who arrives, both satisfied and humble, to offer a billy-goat or a ram to the saint who triumphs over every ordeal.

People come from far, far away, sometimes walking for days on end. There are those who don't even speak the language from here but a different one that's more respected because it's closer to the sacred language.

Those who come from far away don't stay for just a day. With a complete supply of household gear, they camp out for two or three days around the saint's tomb. These are blessed days when the holy place comes out of its tedium and lethargy to shake with interminable and insistent religious recitations. The whole village takes on a new, energetic look. There's a feeling that the villagers are rediscovering their spiritual ascendancy, the prestige of their roost and their drowsy piety. Those who normally never approach the sacred spot, come to catch a glimpse out of curiosity and often wind up by joining in the devout practices. Buckets for the ablutions are brought from every house, old holy books whose worn pages haven't been turned in months go from hand to hand.

The saint's sanctuary is called La-Source-de-la-Vache, for there's a spring very close. As for the story about the cow, it's familiar to all the pilgrims, some of whom have spent days walking to breathe the immutable, invigorating air of holiness.

In bygone days during times of great famine, willful devils would come and steal a cow from the holy man's herd. The animal would be sacrificed, cut up, and divided into piles of meat equal in number to the houses in the village, even before the spiritual master's retinue was aware of the theft. This way every villager was implicated in the sadly remembered business. Hunger had conquered piety. But in the evening, when the mountain people were getting ready to have their delicious dinner, the likes of which they hadn't tasted in months, not one of the housewives could find the string of meat she'd slipped into the earthenware pot, which was only used on special occasions. The peasants spent the night in agony, trembling in anticipation of some monumental punishment, much like the earthquake that had been sent to their ancestors when they were late with their prayer. The next morning, the sacrificed cow was wandering serenely around the village square, nibbling here and there at a sprig of clover or a thistle.

With their extraordinary powers, cows had established the renown of the eminent family forever. The holy man's father, himself no less saintly, his mausoleum a half-day's walk from La-Source-de-la-Vache, saw an elegant traveler arrive one day with a fierce lion from the Atlas Mountains on a leash. The villagers ran home to barricade themselves. The traveler went over to the devout man's house, expecting a huge reaction to the wild beast. Haughtily he asked:

"Will you give shelter to a guest of God?"

"Welcome be to any believer the road brings to us. My house is also yours."

"Where, Your Holiness, may I keep this lion tied up until I leave?"

"Take him to the stable, my son. There's a cow there already who must be getting sleepy. The two animals will keep each other company."

"Did I hear you correctly? In the stable, oh blessed and charismatic man? However, I'm quite fearful for the cow."

"Go ahead, my son. God's powers are boundless.

He alone can decide the fate of his creatures."

During the night, staying up quite late, the two men discussed the events of the world, while the arrogant stranger ostentatiously flaunted his knowledge of things both obvious to, and hidden from, the eye. The marabou was in the position of a pupil, listening humbly and not daring to interrupt the digressions of a well-spoken master. He didn't risk contradicting him even once. When the early dawn began to paint the sky pink, the two completed their first prayers of the day side by side, and then the traveler went to the stable to untie his feline. All he found was a still-warm skin. The cow had devoured the lion.

Humility was the key word in the life of the ancestor in question, which already foretold the fathomless piety of Sidi Maâchou ben Bouziane. When he was still very young, studying in Sidi Berkouk's famous master's circle, the *zaouia*, with fellow students, the simplicity of his clothing, the restraint of his actions, and the modesty of his bearing already set him apart from them. One day when a wealthy believer had donated an enormous five-year old ox to the zaouia the entire student body refused to touch the animal's belly to empty and cleanse it. Maâchou ben Bouziane came forward from among the group, rolled up his sleeves, and went over to the immense ash wood platter where the

entrails and offal lay. The master watched him work
in silence and then, when the young man rose, his
hands smeared with stomach fluids and excrement,
he turned to the other students, many of whom had
already lowered their heads, and said reproachfully
though not in anger:

"He has beaten all of you. He shall be the Master
of the Great Demonstrations."

Maâchou thus began to differentiate himself
from his companions, not by a few odd actions or
some sort of ostentatious behavior, but through
almost total deference and self-effacement. The
young man distinguished himself as much by the
speed with which he absorbed the holy verses as by
his willingness to submit to any test and by his spirit
of self-sacrifice in collective tasks.

The day he left the zaouia, young Maâchou had
already been preceded in his native region by his
reputation as a scholar and a devout man. Having
returned to his village, not yet known as La-Source-
de-la-Vache, he instantly enjoyed the great respect of
the peasants who, his youth notwithstanding, named
him leader of the brotherhood. It was the century
when the Spanish attempted raids on the country's
shores, but Sidi Maâchou ben Bouziane did not
preach a holy war. All he did, each morning after the
dawn prayers, was leave the village armed with his
cane and go off to the sea. There he would strike at a

clump of oleanders for hours on end, until he fell to the ground, exhausted, dripping with sweat and tears. But instead of bitter sap warm blood came streaming out from the bushes. A few week later, public criers came through the villages to let the mountain people know that the Spaniards had just abandoned the last coastal town.

9

To bear witness to the saint's immutable glory, another eight oxen were slaughtered today on the square where the ash trees and eucalyptus grow. Their arms red with blood, men are busy and wasps buzz around taking pieces of meat the size of their own bodies from the chopped-up animals.

The heat lies on the earth like an irremovable stone slab. Today, the sun very quickly reached the sky's sweltering heart, where it came to rest, unconcerned about the discomfort it produces in the people who pant beneath it like oxen under a yoke.

Only the noise of the wasps in flight regulates the furnace nesting in the summer's navel. It's easy for them to slip past the attentiveness of men. Swift and tireless clippers, they pounce on the mountains of flesh in little fighter groups. The men don't even have the strength to chase them off their arms where they come to lick at the coagulated blood and small bits of ground up meat. Perhaps they're too busy, for the axes haven't stopped chopping and the knives keep slashing away. The large leg and neck bones have been disconnected at the joints and the immense oxen, which couldn't be brought down until the villagers decided to make a collective effort, are transformed into almost equal-sized piles in which it's now impossible to identify each animal's original head and limbs.

Very offensively raising and lowering their belly, the wasps cling to the meat. Children have come to prowl around the carnage hoping to get hold of a bladder drained of its urine, which they can change into a lucky balloon. Many other things, too, attract their attention—not least of which is the unusual, festive atmosphere that hangs fixed in the somnolence of the heat wave. It's so magnificent, so exciting to see together in the village square the ceremonial white burnooses and the force that brings the oxen down.

Now that the sun begins a slow retreat toward the horizon, an unbelievable sweetness has settled over the village. Having grown more intimate, shapes and colors have stopped being a threat with their glistening, cutting edges. The men have brought the piles of meat inside and all that's left on the square is the sickly smell of blood and empty entrails, the now indifferent circular motions of wasps and flies. Those villagers who weren't part of the bloody feast have finished their work in the fields or their siesta, and men and children are beginning to fill up the mosque's stone blocks and crumbled walls that now serve as bleachers. As for the women, they must be content to gaze insistently from the safety of a wall or an enclosure. Everybody is waiting for the pilgrims.

It's not long before they show up. The first ones have come from the hamlets up high, from the area of Ravin-de-l'Ombre. They could already be seen from the village a good hour before they arrived. The men come first with a monochrome flag—yellow or orange, it's hard to make out in the late afternoon's fading light—then come the old women, a shapeless bunch of colored fabrics. Echoing in the ravine, their songs can be heard from afar. They rise very high, sometimes dying out when a natural obstacle comes between them and us, then reemerging in open terrain. But soon songs from other directions ring out. Pilgrims flock in from everywhere and yet only two groups can be seen. Those coming from below, from the riverside, are still invisible, their advance toward the village suggested only by the voices growing louder and louder.

The first to arrive are those coming from the direction of Ravin-de-l'Ombre. At the head with his orange flag is a man who limps rather than walks; now and then, the weight of the pole makes him stagger. Nevertheless, he joins the others in their singing while sweat streams down his forehead; his cheeks and lips are trembling nervously.

As soon as the pilgrims enter the village through the upper entrance, Hand Moh Ouali, one of the members of the holy family, runs to meet them. He rushes to the flag bearer, rips the pole from his hands and, returning to the head of the line with the flow of pilgrims, he starts chanting and singing along with them, nodding his head in exaggerated fashion and hopping first on one foot, then the other, as if walking on live embers. In someone so young, his highly archaic clothing and his overstated piety make him look ridiculous. Despite the solemnity of the moment, some people have a hard time containing their laughter at the sight of his enormous turban and his frenetic gestures.

When the group of men has passed, the women follow. Their steps are hesitant and awkward like those of a shackled herd left in the shade too long, then suddenly set out in the bright light of day, bothered by the intense light and by the rough terrain that their legs, no longer used to movement, must cover.

Soon the last pilgrims arrive. And toward sunset everyone gathers in the stone area in front of the sanctuary door of Sidi Maâchou ben Bouziane, holding their emblems like a huge army. The village chief starts to give everyone a profusion of the age-old rhymed blessings that are brought out at every important occasion. Then the people briefly disperse only to gather again around the platters of couscous. It is one of the ceremony's key moments, for the feeding ritual is most important and will later provide fodder for many conversations. The white-haired clerics, waiting to make the altars ring with their chants and trances, focus a great deal on the food— its quantity and quality will determine their zeal as pious vocalizers and dancers. They don't have to be nimble to hop around; on the contrary, what they need is the digestive bulk and drowsiness that sends people into a kind of second state where all restraint, shyness, and modesty fade and then evaporate with the ecstatic groans rising from their chests where the fire flows.

Pious gifts precede the cycle of trances. People, even the poorest wretches, are inordinately generous on these occasions. That's why the chief spreads an immense rug of palm fiber before him and places three baskets by his side so that the pile on the mat will always display the same circumspect quantity. The tone of the blessing ritual bestowed upon the donors is proportionate to the agreed-upon sum. Those who've always been affluent and are spared by the country's Independence, and the new luminaries whom Independence has enriched, come to safeguard their possessions and have them blessed.

The first donor approaches the circle of the devout, throws a brand-new bill of 5000 on the mat. The elderly notables clasp their hands to begin the blessing, but he firmly orders them to be silent:

"This is merely a prelude," he says, "you'll have plenty of time to pray and," as he throws down a second bill, "bless my business."

"May your stores proliferate like mushrooms in autumn and may their numerous drawers receive financial manna like the alveola received honey from the hard-working bees."

"Bless my lands," he says and throws down another bill.

"May the magnanimous God ceaselessly pull back the borders that outline your land and may juice-filled fruit and dizzying buildings grow in close and happy proximity."

"Bless my cars." And a fourth bill falls on the mat.

"May rust, breakdowns, accidents, and everything that impedes smooth driving be kept far, far away from your vehicles."

"Bless my children," he finally says, and a last bill flutters through the air.

"May your offspring belong to the race of those who dominate and may they, in all serenity, enjoy both present and future property with which the judicious God will crown your praiseworthy efforts."

Other donors come by; some ask to have their transport company blessed and protected from the evil eye, some wish for healthy children, and still others want blessings for their emaciated cows or stocky oxen. Not until the last bill has fallen on the voracious mat do other groups start to form circles and chant, first very softly, then the sound becomes one and rises, renting the air, irrepressible in the darkness.

In the vast courtyard before the altar, the trance rumbles like a storm in the chests of the faithful. Every now and then the sacred recitations are supplemented by a deep and modulated moan or an uncontrollable grunt. Heads and chests are already heaving imperceptibly. Then, unsure, a man rises halfway, trembling on his legs like a sick person. But he changes his mind and sits down again. The chanting continues, delivered more rapidly now. And suddenly someone leaps into the middle of the circle with the cry of a wounded animal. He sways wildly from right to left. His eyes are half closed and, shining strangely in the light of the oil lamps, their white suggests complete abandon. Abruptly, he throws his entire body to one side and in the quavering, pained voice of a goat in rut, he blurts out:

"Oh, strength of my youth, what wind has scattered you across the mountains!"

His face is contorted with incoherent desires while its muscles wage a merciless struggle against an invisible demon. Other men stand up and the space created by the chanters is quickly filled with gesticulations, sighs, and groans. I watch the shapes begin to dilute in the light of the oil lamps, to resemble the diabolical, twisted shadows that the flames of a wood fire project on the walls of our house during certain winters. Large numbers of small leaden insects are landing on my eyes.

*

Strange. It's the silence that awakened me. As long as the noise and the dancing continued, they nourished an uproarious, fantastic dream in me. Then my dream became like an unsupported object sustaining itself in the air for a few seconds before taking a heavy fall and breaking. I look around. It's still very dark; in the metallic sky the moon is a bright white shield. The circles of singers and dancers have broken up. And then something shocks me. In the middle of the night the pious old men are stuffing themselves with couscous and meat. A huge bowl with a deep-red sauce is making the rounds between the wooden platters. The old men are eating in silence, transformed into diligent, voiceless animals. They look as if they're storing enough food to last them the rest of the week. Perhaps with age they've acquired the virtues of ruminants, chewing the food they've amassed in their stomachs like cud on days when there isn't much to eat.

As I look around, I see Rabah Ouali slightly

removed from the old ogres in their impeccable burnooses. He, too, is participating in this frenzy of the spoon, together with the less distinguished pilgrims who're not admitted onto the illustrious pedestal of the devout celebrities. Their platter is placed right on the ground instead of on a straw mat as it is for the first group. Still half asleep, I go over to my companion. When he sees me, he gestures and says:

"I've been looking for you. Where did you go? Come, eat, and restore yourself; soon we'll be back on the road again."

The dawn has not yet broken. I look at the cold couscous cemented into compressed chunks by the red sauce. The image makes me gag. I catch sight of a tree very close by and lean my back against it, so I can sleep a few more minutes. But Rabah Ouali wakes me up immediately.

The sun is laying its fire over the hills. We resume our journey toward other hot days and other trances. My brother's bones are waiting for us like a treasure, buried among other heroic cadavers over which orations and praises breed like worms attracted to a rotting carcass.

Book II

1

ven though it was a more than unrewarding life, my brother lived it purposefully at first. For me he began to live a long time ago, on a snowy winter day. I must have been about four. But in ten years' time things have changed so much that today I have trouble believing that what was happening then really did occur. The thicket of prickly pears that used to conceal the village no longer exists, people eat their fill, and tiny airplanes, birds scooped up like little balls, pass by high up in the air laying parallel trails of white vapor.

It was a snowy day. Birds came falling from the sky and lay there, feet in the air, rigid like down-covered stones. We had a meager herd of five goats, whose ancestor—an old black one-eyed nanny goat—could barely walk anymore. But we kept her, we cherished her because of the lovely offspring she had given us and because of her still abundantly-flowing milk.

It was a big day for me, for despite the cold I was given permission to accompany my brother to the pasture (I remember having spent the preceding days dying with boredom, dragging my feet through the gullies that crisscross the village). For people like us, working life starts very early—shepherd at the age of four or five, farmer at thirteen, married with children at seventeen or eighteen. At thirty-five we stop going around bare-headed, wearing "European" pants—we put on a fez and the roomier clothing of our people. We move into the camp of men who expect nothing more from life, who labor in the fields all day and talk with the old men in the evening before the common prayer.

It was a very special day that would be like none that was to follow. In some places the snow was hard as schist, but the sky was a perfect blue with the sun wandering through it like a huge golden coin. It was on that magnificent day where everything I saw took on improbable dimensions, that I discovered the forests and hills of the pasture lands, that I came to know that birds who were too delicate would die.

The world was a frosty mirror that sent shards of light bouncing back. The few sporadic birds were trying out some frightened notes in the top of oak and poplar trees, dark ghosts sculpted on the snow. Forced by the bad weather to stay home day after day, our goats threw themselves in a wild rush on the shrubbery lining the road. My brother had a small strip of bird traps wound around his forearm. When we came to the pasture, he effortlessly dug out some of the soil at the foot of the trees and under the bushes to cover the traps. The shrubs were frozen hard, the sun cut through them, creating pools of light inside.

It was the first time I spent the day "working" with my brother. And it must have been a day when he especially excelled, for I had a hard time recognizing the apathetic, distracted shepherd in this active young man busying himself with his herd and his traps, whistling all the while. Wrapped in rags and with ox hide as shoes, his feet moved with surprising agility.

The first bird caught in the traps was a sickly robin with tousled feathers., Holding it by its two legs as if it were a huge catch, my brother came to show it to me, somewhat disappointed (I don't know why I wasn't allowed to go check the traps with him). It didn't discourage him, however.

"Wait," he told me, "soon it will be thrushes and blackbirds. It's always like that with traps. It starts with the small fry to get things going, then the big ones come flocking in."

Since the big ones and even the smaller ones didn't seem to be in any hurry to make themselves known, my brother decided to pluck the robin who'd now grown cold and wouldn't let go of its feathers without the skin coming off as well.

"You know," he confided in me, "everything in life should be done with patience. But, unfortunately, if we don't want to be too scattered we always have to hurry up. That's why those who are patient are almost never rewarded, even though they are the most deserving. As the saying goes, fortune comes by early in the morning and too bad if you're not up in time. And how about you, what is your biggest concern when you start something?"

I answered him without thinking, but was immediately aware, and extremely proud of, the impact and seriousness of my response:

"I'm afraid I'll die before I'm done."

My brother stood there gaping for a few moments, then came even closer to me and patted my head—a gesture of unrestrained, completely unusual affection.

"That's exactly it," he finally said very quietly. "Just imagine, I have a plan I spend a lot of time thinking about. And every evening before falling asleep, I start shaking with fear, afraid I won't be able to realize it. There's nothing more vulnerable than a human being, you know. When we slip into bed at night are we ever sure that we'll wake up the next morning? An accident can happen just like that. A sheet gets knotted around your head and keeps you from breathing, a chunk of wall that crumbles during the night, a snake that slithers into your bed, and goodbye sunshine, goodbye bread! My plan is not one of the easiest to achieve, but it's not the difficulty of it that scares me, it's more the thought of one of these accidents that come stupidly and unfairly to put an end to our life.

"You may not know it yet, but there's nothing more exhausting and more hopeless than cultivating this damned rocky land of ours. When the plowshare hits against a stone deep down, you can feel your wrists cracking and your heart jumps right into your throat. Those are moments of real torture when for hours and hours I'm holding the handles to plow these sloping fields, to which the oxen cling by some instinct I don't understand, or maybe by a miracle. After a while, dizziness and nausea clutch at my head and stomach, multi-colored stars are dancing in front of my eyes, and a coldness begins to scrape the inside of my chest, it's very uncomfortable. Still, I must go on until evening and again the next day, and the next. That's the only perspective from which I can look with a positive eye at these nocturnal accidents that could shorten our bit of time on earth. When a life is synonymous with so much trouble isn't it more rational to put an end to it? Sometimes God does do things fairly.

"But I've decided—and don't repeat this to anyone because I'll get in trouble, and it's only what you just said that makes me tell you all this—as I said, I've decided to buy one of those machines that move on their own while they plow the land behind them. All you need to do is sit on top in a comfortable seat and let it do its job. I saw them one day when I was passing by the farm of some foreigners. Since then the idea has been consuming me. Can you see what it would mean for our family, for the well-being of us all? I haven't asked what these machines cost yet, but I'm determined to get one. So, as of now, I'm making plans—our herd of goats must increase so we can sell a lot of males, and then I'll have to emigrate to a place where, so it seems, money can be earned without too much trouble. I can already see it all in my head. I'm now in the process of figuring out the best way to break the news to our father. I can't let my courage fail or have the words come out weakly or without conviction. That's all I'm waiting for now. Owning one of these machines is worth any risk for me."

2

One day my brother took me to see the trucks.

The village was experiencing its most senseless, most distressing moments. Each morning brought its new share of implausibility. Thereafter, no one could protect their tranquility from the changes. Not even the oldest and wisest. Some villagers were convinced we were seeing the evidence of the end of the world—especially the morning when Mohand-Oukaci came back from one of his trips with a small box made of metal and fine wood that emitted words and songs. He turned on the marvel without alerting the gathered villagers.

"Someone's head is hiding inside", the best-informed shepherd ventured to explain. But, in view of the size of the box, everyone had to recognize the inanity of such a statement. Still, after a few days of continuous listening, the villagers almost unanimously declared that, far from being an early warning sign of the coming Flood, the new sound effects in their life were an undeniable pleasure. They were memorizing songs, amusing little stories, and in a conversation it wasn't unusual to hear some of the smartest people add, "As they said on the radio this morning...." Obviously, ashamed to have admitted to such frivolity they'd quickly pull themselves together again.

What enthralled us children most of all were the vehicles that started showing up right inside our community. The road that had been cut across the mountains was barely finished when we heard the first reverberations. What a sensational spectacle it was the day we saw three large trucks arrive, one behind the other, honking their horns as they approached the village! Everyone was out and, speechless with emotion, we were able to follow the machines as they advanced toward the village. The paved road didn't go directly through it but passed slightly below where the terrain was flatter. The vehicles stopped when they reached the first houses and then some well-dressed men came out, speaking a language we didn't understand.

So, they were true then, these most unlikely changes the news of which had been spreading for months! Stunned and distraught, on the one hand people were contemplating the diabolical machines and, on the other, everything familiar that would soon alter in appearance and become strange to them. A wind of change and disorientation was blowing over the land, uprooting all that was solid and settled, stamping everything it touched with a seal of unfamiliarity. The well-established perception of sounds, images, distances, and movement was completely shattered inside people's heads. From now on, they reckoned, they might well wake up tomorrow with a tail emerging from below their gandoura, or perhaps see the sun rise when it should set.

The first day the trucks arrived, the men stayed up in the *djemaâ* deep into the night. All afternoon an embarrassed silence had been floating over the gathered villagers. Nobody dared speak, for either they couldn't talk and avoid speaking of such enormous events, or else it wasn't easy to find the right words for the scope and future of such changes. Was it even possible hereafter to utter an opinion that would not then be proven false the next day? But as dusk descended, followed by the night's darkness, people became involved in a discussion, first in a secretive tone and then gradually with greater confidence in their own judgment. Still in the prime of his life but handicapped by his huge belly more than by old age and physical weakness, the village chief spoke exhaustively about a remarkable man, an ascetic, an imam and a poet, who had foreseen all the upheaval we were now experiencing with more, and even more astounding, things to come. At first the words rumbled in his gullet, then they came out of his mouth, spurting forth in greasy breathlessness. He supported his statements by reciting verses the

holy man had composed on the subject. Most of
the verses indicated that those responsible for this
depressing reality were humans who'd turned out to
be impious. The chief stopped talking, panting loudly.
He was so huge, so blubbery, that more than half the
village homes were inaccessible to him because their
doors were too narrow. When he was forced to move
around, there was only one animal that could carry
him on its back—an unbelievably passive, almost-
blind albino mule who let itself be mounted by every
donkey in the region.

The trucks did not return the next day nor the days
thereafter, but the memory of their passing through
continued to plague everyone's mind. One day when
my brother and I were watching the goats close to
the paved road, we heard an engine sound in the
distance. Right away my brother dragged me inside
a kind of grotto amid the cork oaks. "Not every truck
is like the ones that stopped in our village," he said
to me. "There are others that carry armed men who'll
shoot at anything they see."

My brother didn't scare me. All he did was
rekindle an old desire in me, which would sometimes
wane only to revive even more insistently—I've
always dreamed of owning a weapon to shoot at birds
and rabbits. Ahmed, Tayeb, and I had spent days and
days searching and working to produce something of
the sort, but all we'd managed to put together was a

crossbow. The straight branch of a birch tree, its core emptied out, converted into a weapon of tension, didn't satisfy us at all. Only metal fascinated us. In fact, we were dreaming of many objects made of metal—stuff that shoot bullets, machines that moved or flew. We'd spend our time scouring garbage dumps where countless discoveries only sharpened our desire to create and escape. One day we found a rusted bike of which only the wheels, saddle, chain, and handlebars were missing. We carried on, ranted and raved about how the precious relic might be used. We separated late in the afternoon without having come up with the best idea, but we swore we'd come back to the finest of the hypotheses.

It was summer, it was very hot, and with the entire village mired in a sweltering siesta, we devoted our time to a tour of the garbage dumps. Since I didn't own a hat, the sun had tanned me like a tree stump. My mother had started calling me *Akli ouzal* ("noontime black boy"). The only living creatures we'd find among the trash were chickens who were digging holes in which they'd bury themselves halfway to take advantage of the relative coolness of the still-moist refuse. They'd look at us stupidly, their tongues hanging out from the heat like dogs exhausted from hunting game. We knew there were plenty of rats, too, but they'd flee or hide as soon as we began to come near.

Once the trucks had arrived to disturb the calm of our existence, our forays to the dumps stopped. What we'd dreamed of for so long had materialized before our very eyes. Instead of heading for the scrapyards, the three of us would now sit by ourselves in the shade talking about the trucks. One day, Ahmed informed us:

"It seems that the machinery we've seen here is not the best of what's available. There are more powerful ones that can climb hills and pass over trees. That's what Mohand-Arezki said. He claims he's already been inside a truck before."

That was the accomplishment that for several days fostered Mohand-Arezki's superiority. Not one of us boys dared contradict him, for we were all hoping he'd give us specific and exciting details about this dreamed-of ride. While we were waiting, he strutted around among us, stingy with his confidences, content to just throw out some occasional enigmatic allusions to the speed, to the comfort of the seats, and to the wind playing through his hair.

But we didn't have to wait to ignore Mohand-Arezki and his supposed escapade. The trucks began to come to the region again, in large numbers this time. We even realized there were different varieties and we soon managed to familiarize ourselves with the proper name of each vehicle. We overlooked many things—our trips to the dumps, our games with marbles and tops, our snares for turtle doves and woodpigeons. We'd settle in on a mountain pass to watch the trucks arrive. We could see them at about ten kilometers before they reached the village, right before they'd get onto the bridge across the river. Once we saw them at night, luminous eyes in the world's dark sleep. They advanced, drilling the darkness like crankshafts of light. Dumbfounded we watched them, our chests too narrow to hold our leaping hearts. In the intense silence punctuated by heavy breathing, a voice said slowly, hesitantly, pathetically:

"No, what I told you isn't true. I've never been inside a contraption like that."

3

The news that a school would be built made a dramatic entrance into the village. I was in the meadow, deep in the grass up to my waist, thinking about very straight chairs and book bags of brand new leather. The adults assured us the school would change a great many things, both in the behavior and the mental state of the villagers. So I began thinking about everything that was going to vanish—birds and the warm texture of their feathers, wandering clouds and their ephemeral, free-flowing forms, the knotty tree trunks, the familiarity of the herds we'd take to pasture at dawn. Beside it I saw the new life that was to be ours—supplies of crumbly chalk, the plant-like smell of sheets of paper full of pictures, a new language that contorts the lips and makes the voice grow huskier. Geometric mornings of faded sunshine or tamed rainfall; no more fearless cavorting after capricious goats. I imagined the change would take place suddenly one winter morning, moored in the luster of an impartial sun. Robins, larks, warblers, and woodpigeons wouldn't fly off any more when we'd approach—they'd just be embedded like birds of ink in the implacable book of nature.

I was pondering all that with an uncertain feeling where the most contradictory urges collided. I've always been enticed by the unknown, but I sensed that this time around it was going to take the form of invisible bars that would prevent me from continuing my visits to the dump, setting my traps inside shrubbery where the rain didn't penetrate, removing bits of branches to try and make impossible grafts, and going off to shoot the forest's most exotic animals with a secret rifle in my brain.

They came with helmets on their heads and a lot of equipment. They were almost all foreigners. Still, some of them were exactly like us; they said their prayers five times a day and spoke a language that we partly understood.

They did it all, and very quickly, too. Gigantic metal panels were erected on the lot where the school was to be constructed. The sun brutally ricocheted off the metal and a stifling smell of paint hovered in the air.

We often went to watch the men as they worked. Some of the boys would go there just to inhale the wafts of paint, which they loved. One of the construction workers had only one hand, but he was highly skilled and carried on like a mud dauber. His name was Saï; he came not from our country but from a neighboring one. Since he spoke a language almost identical to ours, he'd have long conversations with us while he worked, bent over his crates with bolts, metal plates, and cans of paint.

"Your world is going to change," he told us. "Oh no, not for the better. It's just that the things inside your head will take on other configurations, your dreams will be shaped differently. The purple lymph of the inkwells will tamper with your blood. Birds and helicopters, wool and synthetic cotton, party ribbons and hunter's lassos, entertainment machinery that also serves as devices of torture, there's so much you'll discover that's illusory that you'll never manage to hold the world by its most innocent end again.

"There's no doubt you'll put up a struggle at first, but the mucilage of words is too fascinating. No call for help will clear the wall of deceptive smiles created just to put you at dubious ease. Forms meaning the same thing that destroy each other; other, contradictory forms conceived of to inflict the same torture. They've regulated everything— even the mistakes of nature. They know that burns and biting frost cause exactly the same injury. You'll get to know how to bear death with a smile, how to perpetuate evil as if it were a gift.

"Words have many sides. Have they seduced you yet? Just wait for the images and the devices that go along with them. You'll get to know the coldness of rectangle, glass, and plastic. In the whirlwind of angles and ellipses even the cleverest one of you won't manage to find a hole through which to escape. They will count you, compute you, label you, and the machine will be responsible for attributing an immutable face and a definitive number to each of you. Trees won't speak to you anymore and birds won't brush against you any longer. You'll find out there's nothing more horrifying than one's own image, an image so unbearable you'll want to obliterate it. Do you think I'm thrilled with my face, red from paint, with my truncated limbs? Why don't you go and question the mangled trees about the pain that rises from their still-living roots?"

We didn't comprehend everything he was telling us, for his language included many words we didn't know. Besides, we were sure that he didn't always talk to be understood, but that he was haunted by a talkative demon that rattled on via his mouth. One day he told us:

"The school is about to be finished. But don't think it's going to stay there, inoffensive and benevolent, just to quench the thirst for learning of young shepherds. Knowledge is not pure and clean, it's the color of a truncheon. Ah yes, keep dreaming your dreams of innocent pictures, of words that don't excoriate the mouth, of a fire in the stove in winter. There'll be something quite different to welcome your hunger and your unsuspecting naiveté."

Indeed, the school was soon built. One autumn day other foreigners arrived to take over from the workers. They were clearly much better dressed and more imposing. They left again after a few hours, leaving just one man behind, the smallest one, who was going to be the village teacher. Oh no, he wasn't mean, and the image of precious knowledge inculcated through being beaten with a stick that had inhabited us for so long, soon left the youthful minds. I wasn't admitted to the school because I was still too young. But I would learn to read later and I learned fast, too—that's what lets me describe all this today.

Each evening, filled with wonder, my brother would tell me about the special place with its brick seats (the tables hadn't arrived yet), about the color photographs that opened the walls onto the dream. He told me that from the classroom you could hear the big olive tree rustle, but it wasn't just branches and leaves you would see, there was also a profusion of supernatural colors, small moving ships, and infinite numbers of unfamiliar animals that seemed to have come straight out of the book the teacher would circulate from row to row.

One day my brother brought home a piece of green chalk. He handed it to us to touch, inhale, to feel its texture. He proudly let it make the rounds when the girls next door came over to also have a look. He assured us that unimaginable marvels could be drawn from this bit of smooth rock and that he'd be able to get some other pieces, too. The next day every wall in the neighborhood, every stone, every large rock was covered with dogs, rabbits, flowers, and little green houses.

But the most blessed day was when the picture books arrived. Not everybody got one, only half the class. My brother managed to get one to share with a friend of his, named Akli. He'd keep the book all morning and my brother would get it back early in the afternoon before the herds went off to pasture. We'd go to get the book with a group of five or six of us, made up of my brother, myself, an occasional friend, and the neighbor's daughters. We established a method for taking turns to keep the book overnight. One of our new games, perhaps the most usual one, entailed our sitting in a circle with the book in the center and as the pages were turned we'd name everything we would like to have owned among those lovely objects and images—trees, houses, shops, rakes, plates, tables, cabinets. We saw ourselves with a wealth of priceless treasures. Sometimes the game had us state whom, among the many individuals rushing across the pages, we'd like to resemble. It was almost always the appearance of the clothing that would determine our choice. A fight broke out one day because one of the neighbor's daughters wanted to look like a child who, in everybody's opinion, was a boy.

My brother never joined in this game, first because he thought he was too big for it, but there was an additional reason that he wouldn't tell us. The first time he brought the book home he sat down hastily and started to leaf through it nervously, searching—I was sure of it—for one of those machines that plow all by themselves. Then, looking gloomy, he put the book down and remained quiet for a few seconds.

Many, many things in the book were unknown to us. We could vaguely guess they might be used for eating, sitting down, or moving about. I liked the horses more than anything else; I'd sit and look at them for hours and suddenly they'd break away from the edges of the pages and start galloping through the sleepy midday air. They crossed the silent village, then became lightweight, evanescent, before joining the white clouds, which an invisible carding tool had scattered.

4

Then other pictures arrived. They were more impressive than we could ever have imagined. It was unbelievable! A dog running down the stairs chasing after a man. The whole village was in the classroom, holding its breath, waiting to see the outcome of this manhunt. The women had short curly hair and wore hats, speaking in very delicate voices. And we were listening to it all while the projector purred gently in a monotone lullaby.

What we were being shown defied even the most fertile imagination. The characters' impeccable dress, the interiors of the homes, the women's immodest bearing and shameless behavior, and then—an extraordinary and funny situation—the women were beating the men! But no one dared laugh or make any comment, the moment was too serious and too embarrassing. The audience barely dared to sneeze or wipe its nose.

The projector sounded like a heavy, steady rain. I was very uncomfortable, for after a while I was convinced it really was raining outside. And I thought of the day when I was caught in a rain storm with heavy winds, I remembered with immense fear the sensation of suffocating, something I felt for the first time when someone unexpectedly emptied a bucket of water over my head.

The screening went on for a long time. When our hero's journey ended with his death and a few spectators were audibly sniffling, it was almost night. The classroom spit out the horde of villagers that had come together for such an unusual event. They left in silence, simultaneously astonished by the motionless, completely unexpected journey, and ashamed to have spent a good part of the afternoon being entertained like carefree children. But most incensed of all was the chief, having somehow, disgracefully, missed the hour of the first evening prayer. In a soft voice, he vilified the devilish machine that was turning every believer away from his religious duties and the naive villagers who let themselves be taken in by fanciful images, like blind game into a trap. And had the temptation been even more real, had every possession and pleasure that leads away from the straight and narrow path been made concrete before their eyes, perhaps all of them would have surrendered without a moment's hesitation. Did they really see themselves with the wealth of these foreigners to think they could spend an entire evening leisurely watching such brazen images? Poor misguided villagers so industriously shoveling their way to Hell!

He was seething, reproaching everyone without sparing himself. When he arrived at the mosque, it was not a call to prayer that came out of his mouth but a furious litany that seemed to sting the misled piety of the foolish villagers like a whip.

Back home, I spent the night dreaming of inextricable stairs, rabid dogs, and women with their hair undone.

The villagers would so have loved to pursue the fantastic voyage to these worlds where life is clean and people are well dressed but, sadly, the appliance with the voice of rain didn't purr for weeks. Yet, we kids had stocked up enough dreams and feelings to meet and hold forth on houses, clothing, and women who'd come to tour our mountains for a few hours (we were all under the impression it was longer than that). Arezki Amaouche told us that his father, who had worked abroad for a few years, had among his papers the photo of a woman who looked like the women in the film, dressed in a long jacket like a man and with curly hair. We also learned that the famous argument between his parents, which had turned the whole village on its head and was still remembered, had exploded the day his mother discovered that photo. It was all very intriguing to Arezki. He really liked the photo and every time he saw that his father was about to open his file of papers he'd move in closer to catch a glimpse of the woman with the curly hair. He not only liked her face and her unfamiliar clothing but also the special smell the paper exuded that reminded him of overripe peaches. We all thought his father was really lucky to have lived in that world of dizzying stairs, well-dressed men (at the time he, too, had obviously been "dressed to kill' like them!), and shameless women who weren't even embarrassed to slap you when they felt like it.

"Surely your father knows women with reedy voices like those we saw. That's why your mother was mad."

"They're not women you'd want to know, for they do things one can't approve of. He must live an indecent life to know any women like that!"

Ahmed wanted to articulate something disturbing, but he didn't know how to say it and, quavering, his voice died down. We knew that whatever he'd wanted to communicate was extremely serious and so, after he stopped talking, we observed a long silence. To break the heavy silence that threatened to turn into discomfiture, Dahmane spoke up just to say something:

"Your father must have regretted coming back here."

"One always comes back home," Tayeb replied

sententiously.

The power of the purring machine was immense; the images didn't show just one location, they could penetrate the farthest places with the most extraordinary kind of people. When the projector returned, it showed us a somewhat strange people although one that slightly resembled ours, whose men wore earrings and whose women were draped in a sort of veil-like fabric. The story was interspersed with complicated dances and songs performed in an incredibly refined voice.

I was a little sick the first days the film was shown and was cursing my fever, spending uneasy nights intensified by bitter disappointment and insomnia. It was a new disease, a headache that was to hound me for several years. I felt as if a multitude of unpleasant protrusions were knocking at the inside of my skull. The slightest movement of my head made me feel nauseated—but I never vomited, while an unbearable lump lodged permanently between my throat and chest. The first time the affliction seized me early in the morning while my mother was sitting down, busy kneading a large ball of dough for some cakes or beignets. I was watching the dough take on round fleeting shapes, then suddenly the idea developed in me that my mother was molding the opaque, revolting matter that filled my skull. I started to shriek like a madman and then fainted. The next morning, I felt a little better and two days later I was able to get up. My first obsession was to go see the film. Fortunately, it was still there! Had it left before I could see it, I would certainly have gone mad.

People had seen the new story several times, knew every sequence by heart, and every time they were about to forget a scene or an important detail they'd go back to hear the magic machine purr again. The day of my recuperation, the classroom was still packed. You really had to be resourceful to find two empty bricks to sit on. With leaping heart, I waited for them to close the shutters and for the machine to project its beam of light.

The film portrayed characters who didn't look like the foreigners; some of them even wore turbans like us. But there were many fabulous things such as the elephant that carried men on his back— unfortunately, they showed it only once and too quickly at that. I waited for it to reappear, to no avail. A woman draped in lightweight, gaudy fabric was singing in a sharp birdlike voice. Some villagers were now more confident. They allowed themselves to laugh or openly express their admiration. The purring of the machine didn't cause the old anxiety in me anymore, for it no longer sounded like rain. Suddenly there was a moment of great emotion. The audience was sighing like tormented souls. The moment a man brought a red-hot iron close to the eyes of a child, my neighbor grabbed my arm hard, burst into sobs, and stammered through his tears:

"Now he's going to blind him! He doesn't know it's his own son!"

5

The fear and mistrust on the part of the villagers were not unfounded. The only purpose of the captivating moving images, of the trucks that had arrived ahead, was to prepare us for the arrival of the army. It arrived one day in a concert of roaring and rattling noises, evicted the villagers who lived on the mountain crest, and set up its tents there. The next day, demolition and construction work began simultaneously.

For weeks, the village had already been living in a rather bizarre atmosphere. The adults would converse in all kinds of insinuations and innuendoes. The men would mysteriously go out at night, which was most unusual. They were creeping around the alleyways rather than walking, whispering words to each other while barely taking the time to stop. One night, it was already quite late, the men raised their voices in a unified, powerful song that froze our bones before it gave us a strange sense of well-being, once we became used to it. We stayed and listened, motionless. It was a completely new song. Men who'd said the last of the evening prayers together would sometimes linger outside a bit to chant liturgical passages. This time, however, they weren't singing in the sacred language but in our own. Their voices, rising as if in one voice, were like a slash in the density of the darkness.

Noble land of our ancestors
plundered by the foreigner ...

A man had arrived a few days earlier. He wasn't dressed like the peasants. He went to my Uncle Ahmed's house, where the men of the village followed him a short while later. They spent a good part of the afternoon together, after which the villagers were acting differently than before. The following day the stranger was gone.

It took the soldiers two weeks to set up their camp, while letting us continue our normal existence. One fine day they came down from their height, brutally assembled the villagers to impress upon us, once and for all, that they were now the only masters here—and masters with unlimited power at that. They delivered a threatening speech, parts of which a trembling Ali Amaouche translated. They kept us hoarded in the square for a long time. When night began to fall and a few of the babies orchestrated a wailing concert, the soldier who'd talked the most grabbed his rifle and began to fire into the air. Then, rather than simply let us leave, the troops chased us away.

The side of the mountain crest no longer belonged to us. Harsh, violent crenellated walls had replaced the vegetation's copious greenery. Trees were no more than dwarf-sized trunks where nothing rustled any longer. No doubt, the soldiers must have been scared to death of anything remotely connected to the former state of the crest—the villagers, the swaying greenery, the darkness, the sounds of the wind. They spent their time cutting down trees, eradicating shrubs, frisking men, and pursuing shepherds and their herds. Even the chirping of birds had become unacceptable to them. Armed with a rifle, a soldier was posted permanently between what was left of the trees, with the mission to kill any bird within range. He even took care of the needs of nature as quickly as he could for fear a lucky bird might escape his line of sight. We often saw him rush off to the latrines like a disaster victim, then run back even faster, rifle in hand, ready to fire. His face was flecked with red spots, he was always sweating as if he spent his entire life running. But he was a good marksman. We recognized that when he shot a falcon one day.

After a few weeks, the soldiers started to make our life plainly more difficult. They needed water, wood, food. And they expected the villagers to provide them with all of it, using their physical strength and their herds. That good man Saâdi Ouali who, accused of subversive activities, had already been taken to the military camp many times, saw his stable dwindle under his eyes. His son Mokrane left the house one day with a "herd" of one old she-goat and two kids.

"Better that we're the ones who'll eat them," the soldiers said.

One morning, they came down from their mountain top again to take a census of all the young men who, on the back of their donkeys, were to haul water for them. It was winter. The villagers were gathered in the small covered courtyard next to the mosque and the snow was falling slowly in tiny flakes of very white wool. Crushed by the still-life's silence and rigidity, I was there, among the adults. Emboldened by hunger, a robin came and sat on the red roof of the mosque where it stayed for a long time, as if it knew the people were so thoroughly disciplined they wouldn't even hurt a bird anymore. The soldiers' blunt words, which I didn't understand, carved thin lines into the silence, which then quickly closed up again, becoming solid as stone. The voice of the man who was translating was less confident.

My brother was one of the young men selected to haul water. I can see him still, coming home one night, his face red and his hands blue from the cold. He crawled into a corner and began to weep quietly. That upset me, and it took everything I had in me not to start crying as well. It was the first time I ever saw my brother weep, for although his existence hadn't exactly left him without any reason to shed tears, he knew how to absorb life's most bitter blows calmly.

From that day on he became a different person. It was as if his tears had purged an inertia, a passivity, that was festering in his deepest self.

Winter had never been so sad or so cold. We weren't even allowed to go into the fields to gather dead wood—the village was surrounded by barbed wire. People were living a silent nightmare rather than a sense of calm. What bothered me most was that our new situation of confinement removed any possibility for me to set my traps beneath the bushy shrubs where rain wouldn't penetrate. But soon I grew less sad, for the birds—robins, woodpigeons, nightingales, and wagtails—swooped down on the village, seeking a bit of warmth on rooftops and in courtyards. So then I placed my traps just behind the house at the foot of the little mound of olive pits where birds would come picking; it was a stroke of luck that the olive press was so close to our house.

My brother's behavior became mystifying. He was often gone from the house, for long periods of time and at the most ungodly hours. I surprised my parents many times when they were involved in a heated discussion, the topic of which I felt sure was the change in my brother's conduct. When I'd

approach, they would suddenly fall silent or clumsily
try to change the subject. Besides, everyone in the
village had learned to live differently. Words no
longer had the same meaning, greetings no longer
carried the same weight, and bonds of family or
friends no longer encouraged the same relationships
as before. And one fine day the entire population,
children included, knew that some of our men were
in the mountains waging war against the foreign
occupiers. Neither Chérif Ourezki, nor Moh-Tahar,
nor Ali Ouahmed, nor Hamou Méziane were now
part of the village, which awakened each morning
diminished by one young man. We'd wait two,
three days for his reappearance and then we stopped
waiting.

As soon as the intense cold was gone, Ahmed
and I began to meet again. We'd sit down beneath the
big fig tree where in the summer the chickens sought
shelter from the sun. The tree looked more like a
tree's skeleton with its nude intertwined branches,
but its trunk hid us from view and we felt safe there
to speak of the most audacious things. The fighters
in the mountains were our favorite topic. Ahmed
assured me they were very tall, they could pass over
trees and houses. Every one of them could hold his
own against ten foreign soldiers. I didn't challenge his
words but, still, they did seem a bit exaggerated, for
I was thinking of Moh-Tahar and Hamou Méziane,

making every effort to imagine them in their new status as supermen. Clearly, as soon as we were a bit bigger we, too, would have to go into the mountains.

One day, the soldiers allowed us to go to the fields to let our herds graze and take a look at our trees. Spring was about to burst forth and the flowers on the apricot trees were already turning into little green fruits. The entire village was in uproar. Axes, clippers, and scythes were being primed.

We all left at the same time, men and goats together. Not one family in the village had kept a pair of oxen. The new measures imposed by the soldiers permitted us to keep only goats and donkeys. People were scattering through the meadows like kids, each heading for his own field or orchard. It had been so long since I'd buried myself in the vegetation, since I'd felt the grass's rough tongue and the crumbling clumps of earth on my hands and legs. My brother entrusted me with the goats. I knew somehow this was a particularly serious day and so I didn't even think about setting any traps—besides, I'd left them at home.

My brother was very busy in the field. It wasn't until the evening, when the sun spattered the color of pale blood across the mountains above the river, that he joined me. We went home together. He spoke to me as he'd never done before. True, my brother was ten years older than I, but never had he shown such protective support and maturity. As he talked, the forests, birds, olive trees, violence, blood, and forgiveness took on other contours, a different density, to my eyes. Listening to him, I understood that one could simultaneously be both naked and rich, clever and humble, strong and generous, impressive and wretched. For a moment I stopped being afraid of the foreigners whose heavy boots came by each day to stomp on our dreams and our tranquility.

"One day, all this will be nothing but a bad memory that will be eclipsed by greater demands. It's not me saying it, but men much wiser than I. Our way of being will also change. We won't be using our powers to tear each other apart anymore. The hatred that balloons in our hearts when a neighbor is successful at something or when someone has even a tiny particle of land more than we, that hatred will make room for more generous feelings. To reach that point we must accept that for a while blood and death will be our companions. It's like the tree we graft. We shouldn't let the oozing of the sap make us forget the promise of the fruit. Blood is sometimes needed to irrigate the fruit's flesh and provide it with the redness that perfects it."

When I woke up the next morning, my brother was not at home. Nor was I to see him the next day or the months that followed. When I sought refuge beneath the fig tree to talk about serious matters with my friend Ahmed, we now would speak of him as well. I knew he'd become a very tall man who could leap over trees and walls. And I was very proud of him.

Book III

1

From my mother I inherited an invaluable reflex—catching a louse in the thickest hair or in the deepest darkness at the first try. I remember that during the war her motherly hand would twist itself in my hair or on the seams of my clothes and pull out the teeming bugs with fierce precision in the middle of the night. The hand would come down on my skin and leave it again with a gentleness that in no way showed, or even let one guess at, her murderous intentions for these little creatures. I'd often fall asleep before her pleasingly massaging fingers had left my body.

The dexterity of that hand has passed into mine. It's been very useful to me for, during our wanderings, my body was crawling with parasites. It was nighttime when I first noticed it. We lay down under the open sky as usual. It was a very mild night, but I couldn't fall asleep. Suddenly I felt an itch on my hairy skin; a few seconds later, my stalking fingers came back with an adult louse. I soon noticed it wasn't alone. The war I declared on the colony kept me busy for a good part of the night.

We'd already left our village quite far behind; I now feel as if I left home centuries ago and am fated to travel forever. How vast this world can be! And then to realize that I haven't even left that part of the country where people speak our language. One day we approached a few entirely barren hills and I thought: this is the Sahara. But I knew it wasn't so.

The heat is oppressive; we've moved away a considerable distance from the shore and are now unable to stop for a nice dip in the sea. We must pursue our struggle against the road and the sun. Dusk is the only moment that seems like a blessing to us, but I'm apprehensive of the coming of the night itself, for with it comes a sadness that borders on anxiety. I'm bored with Rabah Ouali in the evening, and anxious ideas assail me. I think of being imprisoned inside a very white house, I think of paralysis and other infirmities, of old age and death. I think about being like Rabah Ouali one day and that then I will have no reason at all to hang onto life, to this world.

Certainly, it's the furnace of noon that raises and fuels all these crazy ideas inside my head, which then surface at night, ripe and cold like truths that can be touched. The sun is benevolent in appearance only, but it's what causes illusions and mad thoughts to ferment inside us. I've always preferred winter. It's the season that makes seeds germinate and prepares the surprise of flowers, that awakens the elements and asks them to start moving and whirring, that drives the chilled, scrawny birds to our homes.

The grass has bloomed twice this year. In December, when an unexpected spring was born in the middle of a sunny spell following a heavy rainfall, and then again in March after other downpours. But nothing is left of this double flowering. It's almost as if in this land of liquid sun the spring and the balmy seasons have never shared the weather.

The sun bores like a drill. It forces you to immobility, to a slow and silent death. We walk to escape from it, to accelerate the rhythm of the hours, to hasten the disappearance of the eye of fire. Sometimes the heat is so oppressive that all the water of my body drains away, all the sounds of midday, which goes on forever, come together to beat on my ears, while my eyes are pulled away into a vertiginous dance and no longer see what they need to see. That's when I want to beg Da Rabah's indulgence, ask him to stop in the shade of a tree, drop down there, down on my belly to drink the shade and stay that way until the world ends—until a season of water and coolness comes to rip us away from the furnace.

But torpor scatters my thoughts and obliterates my will. What ruminates inside my head must cut across menacing infernos before it reaches my mouth and finds its expression there. And so I content myself to dream secretly of a respite that resembles death, in the sweet shade of a tree so broad it seems to be the world's parasol. Besides, even if I'd spoken up, I wonder if Rabah Ouali would have given in to such frivolous and defeatist arguments. You don't think seriously of stopping in the middle of a heat wave when your task is one of the most noble, when a skeleton's spirts are champing at the bit somewhere, waiting for the hands of deliverance that will take them back to the landscapes and familiar sounds of their childhood. Somewhere a skeleton lies waiting for honors to be bestowed upon him. For the dead see us, hear us. Let no one speak ill of them or desecrate what they've left behind on the earth of the living. Their vigilance (and perhaps their lack of discretion) serves them to leave the hereafter.

Poor living humans, I would sometimes think, who're not protected from earthly misfortunes, from bad weather, from famine, from the abuse of occupying forces, or even from the vindictive gaze of their own dead. That's why this country's living like to talk about death so much. It safeguards them from so much destruction. I'm convinced that if the villagers were able to live like the foreigners or even in simple ways like the inhabitants of Anezrou, the little town we came through, they'd stop being in love with death and maybe even stop thinking about it. They would enjoy the feasts, the relaxation, the calm that right here on earth Paradise holds in reserve for them. Furthermore, the villagers must be deluding themselves; I wonder what they've ever done to deserve Paradise—with their stinginess, vindictiveness, jealousies, and cruelty! And I don't really see why, instead of other people, they should be going to Hell, since their life here on earth has been merely a Hell in disguise, after all. I'm sure that the truly aware must be consumed by this dilemma. They know all too well that Paradise is no achievement; only they don't dare admit to each other the possibility of going to Hell, or even of going nowhere at all, something even more problematic. But they think about it anxiously. That's why they show such admiration and envy for those who died in the war. For them the question has been resolved—Eden awaits them with wide-open doors. Not because they allegedly did good deeds on earth, not because they allegedly prayed too much or gave alms, but merely because they died while defending the soil of their homeland. If they've been given so much credit, it must certainly be so that, in turn, they who hear us, watch us, and judge our actions, will intercede on our behalf with those who weigh our souls in the Hereafter.

But for now, with this noontime heat focusing its flames on us, I think the greatest piece of luck the happy dead enjoy is to be escaping from the heat's anvil. For everyone seems to agree that Paradise is cool and verdant; it doesn't exasperate its residents with excessive cold or excessive heat. When they fall asleep in the summer beneath trees whose fruit is of all seasons, the leaves are transformed into dancing palm fronds to fan them gently. What an enticing perspective! Fortunately, we are not heathens, and fortunately, too, God has allowed us to be born in this religion that He has blessed.

Still, before arriving in the Hereafter—and I admit I'm not in any hurry—we must pass through interminable summers that pour their molten metal over us and fasten sparks to the air that blind you if you're not careful. Despite his endurance, our donkey, too, is crying out his pain. His nostrils widen to grunt with the effort and from time to time raucous, almost human groans come from his throat. Apparently, among the three of us Da Rabah is in the best shape. He has lost his volubility now, but his straight bearing and his steady pace do not give any indication they're forced. Perhaps that's why I never dared communicate my plea to let us sink into the indolence of a boundless repose in the shade of a tree—until the arrival of a milder season. I sense my companion is quite indifferent to such a desire. And I can foresee the blast of moralizing—the youth today...when I was your age.... Or else, he may not have even understood my request and I would have gotten off with a paternalistic, ironic sermon about my notions of virility, stamina, and patriotic missions.

My only option is to keep my Paradise of shade and coolness inside my head where brooks rustle, thick foliage swishes, and the wind blows through the reeds. I think of the winters that can be so cold at home, the sad music of the wind bestowing a heavenly sweetness on our sleep and an indolent term of bending and stretching on time.

But the crushing weather scatters my memories. I wonder if this country has ever known a season of gentleness and forgiveness, a season that with floods of water can lash and cleanse faces devastated by the summer.

The earth is nothing but a powdery skeleton crumbling under the sun and the travelers' steps move through dust as fine as smoke. Sometimes the donkey's hooves give off sparks when they touch the stones. One evening Rabah Ouali breaks his monastic silence:

"Tomorrow," he says, "we'll be in Boubras. It's our last stop before Bordj es-Sbaâ. We should rest there a while. Until now we've really been overdoing it."

2

I never could have imagined a city like Boubras. It's considerably larger than Anezrou and there's no way everyone who lives there can know everyone else. We arrive in the middle of the day in the scorching heat, because Boubras lies enclosed between mountains and has a much less temperate climate than Anezrou. Still, regardless of the heat, the traffic is frenetic, men and honking cars going in all directions. How do people manage to find their way in this ocean of shouts and motion? The turmoil borders on the vertiginous. How can they meet those they want to meet, find the things they're looking for?

Judging by all appearances, however, the city's inhabitants aren't bothered by the constant chaos or the many intersecting streets. They walk along thoughtfully, looking as if they know exactly where they're going and what they want. They're not crazed, distracted, pushed, or overwhelmed by the tall houses, the innumerable cars, and the streets that all look alike.

We left our donkey at the entrance of the city where we tied him to an old olive tree. A good thing, too, for we would have looked like pretty peculiar beasts among all those noisy cars and well-dressed people. Already my pants, home-made by my mother, will surely make me look a little sheepish with its somewhat sagging crotch. Adding a donkey on a leash would quite simply have been untenable. Fortunately, Rabah Ouali sometimes faces the facts. I would have done anything for my clothes to vanish from my body and thereby to stop lugging around my origins, my social class, and my embarrassment, which betray me like an open book for the eyes of passersby to browse. Just to be like everyone else without a sarcastic finger pointing at you to be tortured. Just to be like everyone else is also Rabah Ouali's ambition. And to get there, if only for a moment, he's prepared to do something crazy. It's clear to me now that in that defiant step of his he's heading for a café, cutting through the crowd running in every direction, with me right behind him.

Some earthly pleasures can't possibly have an equivalent in any above or underground paradise. Among them is the pleasure of sitting in a chair, legs stretched out, watching the perpetual motion of the street where people look like restless flies.

When the waiter arrives, Rabah Ouali says:

"Lemonade! A whole bottle."

Once the waiter leaves, he winks at me with a look of superiority and explains we're better off with a bottle. If we ask for a glass each, we would be paying the same amount as for a bottle, which holds four glasses. I'm parched and silently praise my companion's shrewdness. The lemonade is very sweet and feels nice in the throat and nose. We use all our available time to thoroughly enjoy the chairs in the shade, more comfortable than any stones, slabs, or mats that have served as my seat until now.

Flies zoom around, come down to lick the moist circles left on the table by the bottoms of our glasses. Customers talk about the precipitous departure of the foreigners, what they've left behind, and the art of buying buildings and trucks for almost nothing. One of them says:

"As soon as I got into the car I let the butt of my gun show from my pocket. So the examiner looks at me and says: 'Which license do you want—the regular one, the one for heavy trucks, or the one for public transportation?' 'All three,' I said."

Another starts to talk.

"God came to our aid. Even when we were dying we died decently and in order with the Creator, while they—we'd find their abandoned corpses, their pants soiled with excrement. We were eating acorns and grass but we held out and, when the battle began, our blood turned into boiling lava and the enemy ranks would thin out like a wheat field under the scythe."

The war that had just ended is central to the discussion, but the customers also talk about the present, how to obtain goods and jobs in administration. It's so nice to listen to the sound of the conversations, to imagine all the interesting things and situations they're dealing with. There are so many happy people on earth it seems, talking about trucks, shops, buildings the same way we in the village talk about a herd of goats or a wooden plow.

Time passes, and I'm deeply grateful to Rabah Ouali for prolonging this extraordinary rest in comfortable seats within the range of discussions that dish up the finest possessions in the world as if they were routine and innocuous things. How lucky these city people are! They sip lemonade or tea, speak loudly about the most unlikely subjects, and laugh uproariously without worrying about bothering anyone else. They're not concerned with the discretion and mistrust that villagers have, which oblige them to watch their tone of voice, the movement of their lips, and their footprints.

When we leave the café, our limbs restored and our mind relaxed, we walk around the fabulous city with its shop windows displaying an impressive array of clothes, utensils, boxes in all sizes, and incredibly beautiful shoes in many different styles. Smaller stores offer piles of tiny objects used to embellish houses, repair shoes or stoves, make sieves, and sew packsaddles or clothing.

It's become quite late; houses, trees, and objects are silhouetted in oversized shadows. It's even sweeter now to stroll through the city but Rabah Ouali's presence next to me feels like a constraint. I would have liked to go inside a department store and look at, or even touch, some expensive looking merchandise. I begin to realize that even rather small boys permit themselves this divine pleasure. Besides, they're free to do a lot of things since they're able to move around all alone without getting lost in the maze of streets and the deafening chaos.

I wonder if these kids really are like my friends and me in the village. Are they made of flesh, deprivation, and fear like us? Do their parents beat them? Their sisters must be very pretty. How do they eat, sleep? Do they have abject natural needs, as we do? No, I wouldn't think so.

At one point, two boys stood before me, pointed at me, and laughed. Do they like me? I wish they were my friends, especially the younger one whose eyes, mouth, and chin look like those of a girl. I'd give anything to see him every day, let him know how much I like him, take him by the hand and bring him along to play marbles and set traps with me. I'd show him thickets that only I know, swarming with birds like larvae. I'd protect him from everything, I'd face the worst dangers for him, I'd fight adults to defend him or just to please him.

They stay next to us for a long time and then, from the way they look at me and burst out laughing, I realize they sure don't have my best interests at heart. All my affectionate plans destroyed. I'd like to move on quickly now to get away from these heartless boys, but I have to adjust to Da Rabah's stride and be exposed to the sarcasm of the two rascals, whom I've really never wronged.

When we reach the café where we were before, I notice it's teeming with customers, both inside and on the terrace.

"We'll just sit a bit longer before we take to the road again," Da Rabah says to me.

We catch sight of a small just vacated table. The waiter passes by twice without Rabah Ouali signaling him. I understand that having two lemonades in one day is too extravagant and beyond the call of my old companion who decided to go to the café only because he saw so many people there and assumed the waiter might not notice us.

But then an older, almost elderly, man comes over and sits down at our table. Having looked around before, he noticed our table was one of the least crowded. He sits down laboriously, murmuring and mumbling pious invocations as old people are wont to do. But he has no prayer beads, thus breaking with the fashion of flaunting one's religion born from that wind of false devotion that has blown across the land. Everyone who aspires to social and hierarchical climbing has a small visible set of prayer beads and spends his days muttering; it's true even of young people and of those individuals who are a million miles removed from any religious devotion.

After a few minutes, the old man starts a conversation:

"The city is unusually lively," he says. "Remember the calm here just two weeks ago?"

"We're strangers here," Rabah Ouali answers.

"What do you mean, strangers! Can anyone be a stranger in a country that's gone back to the religion of God and is in the hands of believers?"

"What I mean is that we're just passing through. We arrived not too long ago and soon we'll be on the road again so we can make it to Bordj es-Sbaâ by tomorrow."

"And you're traveling by night?"

"Yes, a good part of it, it's cooler and the full moon is as bright as daylight."

The man falls silent for a few seconds as if to make an important decision and then says:

"You'll stay with me tonight. You are my guests. God has sent me riches and I'd like every believer to share them with me."

The suggestion leaves us baffled. Rabah Ouali reflects. He's trying to guess the nature of the trap the stranger may be setting for us. But the old man has a really attractive face and it's very hard to read any malevolent ruse in it. Furthermore, taking a close look at us should be sufficient to know we couldn't entice any bad intentions. So we accept the invitation. It makes me feel strange. And while Rabah Ouali and Moh Abchir—the name of our benefactor—converse, I begin to think about a clean house with many rooms, a warm and copious meal, and unfamiliar objects whose looks alone are restful. I have an intense feeling of security and well-being. I feel weightless, invulnerable, drifting above hunger, thirst, cold, and anything that hurts or plagues the flesh. The world seems nice and warm to me, full of clean scented linen, succulent dishes, and people brimming with concern. It's a feeling I used to have when I was very small, certain summer evenings when flights of swifts came streaking through, evenings when the air was very gentle, and I knew that a fine cake was baking at home.

I heard snatches of the conversation unfolding between my table companions. It was mostly Moh Abchir who spoke.

"We were all born poor and the war has been a trial for everyone. Who would have thought that this country's sons would one day be able to regale themselves with all the riches this land so generously distributes? Who would have thought that all the goods to be seen on our country's surface would come back to us? Houses with running water, with light that goes on simply by pressing a button, cars, trucks, stores, what mother's son would have imagined all this would one day be ours?

"I'll tell you. I used to live in a hamlet about twenty kilometers from here, where I had a little stone house, a donkey, and three goats. I told you, what made us equal before God was our nakedness and our suffering above all. I was afraid to die destitute, for life is so very short! We don't even have time to take the revenge we'd like. But here it is, God always ends up by manifesting himself. The foreigners leave without further ado and everything here becomes legally ours. I'm not one to hesitate. Hardly is our sovereignty proclaimed when I take my oldest son with me, that is to say the oldest of the ones I have left, in a few hours we cover the twenty kilometers that separate us from the city where I batter down the first closed door I see before me. It's a lovely house with several rooms; I go in one door and don't even know which one to leave by. And such treasures inside! Beds, cabinets, chairs, tables, dishes.

"I leave my oldest son there, go back to the village, and the next day the whole family moves in. I left the donkey with a relative but didn't have any time to sell the goats; in the garden of the house I built a small stable with reeds and sheet metal, and every morning I take them out to graze somewhere in the area around the city.

"It would have taken me three lifetimes of hard work to acquire everything I found inside the house. But, as I say, when the hand of God releases its gifts it's boundless. All that wealth in the hands of heathens—it was so unjust, and one day it had to stop. It's true that foreigners have the perishable goods of this world and we the eternal pleasures of the hereafter. But there are injustices that must be rectified on earth itself. Otherwise human beings— poor creatures of flesh, greed, and foolishness—take leave of their senses and stop believing in fairness forever.

"I not only found what we needed to eat, sleep, and sit as only kings do, but I also discovered small crates for a variety of uses—one makes music and songs, another makes ice, and yet another does laundry! But the most intriguing of these boxes produces talking images. The one and only time we turned it on, we saw men and women kissing each other on the mouth. Foreigners really do have some shameless, depraved tastes! When we saw those disgraceful scenes, we couldn't find enough exits to quickly leave that room of infamy and damnation. For a moment I thought it was my punishment for having violated an unknown home. We never dared to go near that diabolical box again, for we couldn't know what it might hold in store for us.

"I can certainly say that I've been incredibly lucky. Some who've left their village for the city are perched like birds in cage-like buildings. I've lived off the land and have stayed close to it. My house is surrounded by good, fertile soil. But foreigners are frivolous. All they thought of planting in such fine earth are fragrant flowers and plants. I've started pulling that out and can already see the onions, carrots, and turnips such rich soil will give me in the fall."

In the evening we leave with Moh Abchir. We enter his house and find ourselves in a spacious room with a long table. There are many chairs but Moh Abchir's wife is sitting on a sheepskin on the floor.

I feel very comfortable inside these impressive walls under the heavy gaze of the large dark-colored furniture. I don't know why, but I start thinking about the picture book my brother once brought home from school, about the impression of clarity and cold that came off the pages and assailed us. It isn't long before the room is taken over by the countless progeny of the master of the house. It's the dinner hour I'm impatiently waiting for; hunger had dug long hallways inside my head and my mind was roaming around in there, speculating on all the delicious dishes one eats in the city. I know they're prepared in a very complicated way. I'm thinking of large chunks of meat, dried beans, flour and eggs, hot peppers, and thick sauces, all of it combined in such a way that you get blends as puzzling as they are tasty.

But when dinner was put on the table it put an end to all my dreams and speculations. The dish consisted of large balls of semolina cooked in a chickpea sauce just the way it's prepared in the mountains.

After the meal another conversation ensues in which I don't participate. The war against the occupier is central to every current conversation in the country and I don't see how I can interfere in such a grave and grueling topic. Rabah Ouali, whose terseness and effusions are equally unpredictable, is in rather good form this evening. He begins to take credit for ventures he has, as far as I know, never achieved, to recount experiences he has undoubtedly never had. It's not so much to give himself status, I figure, but more to counter our host who is a smooth talker.

"My oldest son," he tells us, "went into the resistance early on. I can assure you he did so honestly, without expecting any reward, for he never lowered his forehead to the ground to make amends before his Creator. Instead of teaching him humility, the harshness of our life led him astray. He didn't believe in either Paradise or Hell. He used to say that real problems are of an earthly order. Today I don't even know where his remains are buried—if they're anywhere at all. So I console myself for having lost one son, but I will not accept having lost him for no reason. I need to take my share of this world's riches so my son doesn't brood in that Hereafter in which he didn't believe. They don't scare me, those gentlemen who're loaded down with all their stripes, who want to take everything for themselves...."

I don't know how the conversation ended, I only remember they brought us to another room to sleep. It had lamps with a pale light, a gigantic closet, and a big bed shaped like an uncovered crate. Da Rabah and I slip inside, making the bed sway gently. I say goodnight to my companion and fall asleep right away.

The following morning, when the master of the house comes into our room, we're already up. He insists we have some coffee before we go back on the road. We sit down around the long table again. After finishing the coffee, we get up to leave. Then our host begins to rummage through a stack of objects heaped together in a dirty sheet. He takes out a flashlight and a leatherette saddlebag. He hands them to us and says:

"We must know how to share the riches the divine hand has poured out over us."

3

It's almost evening when we arrive in Bordj es-Sbaâ. Our unplanned encounter with Moh Abchir had altered our schedule considerably. We should have left Bourbras the evening before and then walked six or seven hours before stopping to sleep.

The sun hits us sideways, its rays enjoyably tickling our eyes and body. It doesn't seem like summer. The air smells of warm, dry flowers. Amid such sweetness how can you think about a skeleton, even if it's your own brother's? You'd rather get undressed, let the fragrances caress you, rub you down to become fully aware of its vitality, to feel more alive than ever, to enjoy each minute of the twilight serenity, which infuses everything.

A large city, Bordj es-Sbaâ is situated in a dry region. The small mountains around it are almost denuded, just dotted with dwarf-sized green tufts separated by chalk-white spaces. I've never seen a landscape like this before, the heights with their gentle scattered tops over which the approaching dusk spreads an intense blue light, motionless and cold as stone. There are almost no trees in the city, its houses are very old and drab but the evening's luminous sheen swathes them in artificial radiance and good will.

Thanks to my fatigue and my hurry to get here I find the city attractive and restful. It's plunged in shade, but the sun still dawdles lazily on the peak of the highest hills.

For me, evening has always signified a stop, resting there where a subdued fire is preparing the surprise of hot cake and steaming coffee. Time loses its arduous overly long span, and nothing distresses me.

One spectacle strikes me here—herds of donkeys roam around freely, apparently without any owner. And then to think that the farmers on our mountains must work for months or even years just so they can afford one donkey! When I tell them that upon my return, they probably won't even believe me. The sight of all these wandering animals pacifies Rabah Ouali.

"The donkeys around here," he says, "don't look very different. I think we can safely tie ours up outside."

We entered the city by the most accessible side. The mountains are in front and on both sides of us. The one facing us has an exceptionally gentle ascent and, with its broad splotches of white rocks, looks like a sleeping animal. The sky and the city's light have a unique luster; its calm silence penetrates my

every pore and moves inside me agreeably. Here I
completely forget the funereal mission that is mine.

The inhabitants of Bordj es-Sbaâ don't speak
our language. Suddenly I recognize the air's lively
gleam and the dusk's sweetness—we're not far from
the vast area of sand and palm trees. I would so have
loved to see dromedaries but, regrettably, there aren't
any in the city.

Rabah Ouali asks a passerby where the hammam
can be found and then we head toward the town's
dense center that overlooks the wide road from which
we came. We go into a building that resembles the
mosques you find in cities—the same entrance that
ends in the shape of an arc, the same tiles on the floor
and sides decorated with interlacing patterns. The
only difference with the mosques is that here there's
no carpeting on the floor. Sitting behind a table at the
entrance, a man dressed in a shirt and a simple piece
of fabric around his hips receives us. Rabah Ouali
and he talk for a moment, but I don't understand
what they're saying. Then my companion takes out
some money, which he hands to him. I now surmise
this is where we're spending the night.

We go back into the street; the air has cooled.
Our donkey is still tied up on the side of the road
below. From the saddlebag we take a loaf of bread
and the watermelon we bought in Boubras. We sit
down on the ground and indulge ourselves. Walking

in the evening's brisk air has made me very hungry. The watermelon quenches my thirst so I don't need anything to drink.

The street is practically deserted, the rare person we run into is warmly wrapped in a burnoose. I'm getting tired and cold and am very happy when I recognize the hammam by its arched door. The same fellow sits enthroned behind his desk but now he's draped in a sheet that, like a coat, comes down from his shoulders. He looks like an unruly corpse whose head refuses to become part of the shroud.

We press on and I see the huge badly-lit room with about fifteen men lying on mattresses placed right on the floor. It's a very imposing sight. I'd heard people speak about hammams before but this is the first time I actually see one. The men, horizontally aligned, don't inspire any great confidence in me. They all seem like hobos who have no relations and somehow, pathetically, ended up here. Their proximity bothers me. The man draped in the sheet shows us a double mattress and we cautiously bed down. The better places next to the wall have already been taken and the mattress assigned to us is in the middle of the room. A simple thick cotton sheet serves as blanket, for none of the sleepers has taken off his clothes. Besides, there's no place to hang them, not to mention the fact that these men wouldn't have much faith in their companions in adversity.

I try to overcome the self-consciousness this lack of privacy is producing in me and close my eyes. But my wide-awake mind is on guard. As I close my eyes I try to imagine I'm all by myself in my berth. But snoring, a cough, or a whispered conversation bring me back to reality.

The atmosphere is very heavy, a combination of sweat, the smell of tobacco, and lack of ventilation. I push down on my eyelids, which are gaping on their own now as if under the pressure of minuscule coils; I'm abusing my imagination; and all of it make my temples pound wildly and my body ooze sweat from every pore. I'm wary. I'm beset with all kinds of fears. I listen to the minutes fall like heavy, menacing drops—timeless because so slow.

Every now and then drowsiness overpowers me, but as soon as the apprehension of danger pulls me from my stupor, sleep vanishes with big strides. I wonder if I'll ever fall asleep. Try as I may, my senses are vigilant, anxious, being tested. Now it's no longer sleep that preoccupies me but the daybreak. Since I dozed off repeatedly, I've no idea how much time has gone by. The weak but constant light of the hammam gives me no hint. All it does is blur the torturous drip of the minutes. I start to hope that dawn won't be long in delivering me from this waking nightmare.

Just when I was about to despair of ever sleeping

again, just when I had decided to patiently await the light of day, sleep came. Heavy, infallible like a bludgeon.

I'm back in my native region, more precisely in Bouharoun, as our field is called. It's a very cold winter and I continue with a dream that began I know not when. There's an impression I have, which often recurs in my dreams, where I pursue an adventure begun on previous nights. This time I'm all alone in the field, without even our herd of eccentric goats. What am I doing here? I don't seem to have a particular task. I'm as free as the icy air flogging me. Yet, I'm not happy about it at all. A threat's looming presence dampens the taste of this freedom. I'm firmly convinced someone or something is after me and that I've come here to escape it. Terrified, I inspect the surroundings. I also know that somewhere in the thicket I've set a bird trap and am supposed to check it but I can't move in that direction as my stalkers could very well be hiding there. And so I roam the fields, probably expecting help of some sort or a person who'll explain what it is I'm dealing with. But I can't stop constantly glimpsing at the bushes where my trap is set; and I never figure out whether I do so to protect my trap from thieves or to see my pursuers catch up with me.

I'm sitting under the fig tree with its purplish black fruit when I notice a figure creeping toward the bushes. For an instant I stop being scared and very loudly yell in his direction. The figure gets up: it's my brother. He comes over to me and says:

"I wanted to test your watchfulness. There are a lot of thieves around."

"I don't know why I'm here. Someone must be after me."

"No, of course not. You came to the field to see the lizards and, since it's winter, you may have to wait for a long time."

The cold is sharper than before. Before, when I used to watch the goats in this same place, it often made me cry. But now that my brother is here I feel calmer and happy. I love winter. Bits of blue sky peek through the gashes in the clouds. I see now that the tallest of the mountains around the village is covered with snow. Now and then the sun bounces off it as off a mirror. The cistus and mastic bushes are weeping shimmering tears of rain. I hear a few birds sing.

Suddenly a large green lizard comes out of the bushes. He's unusually large, but I know it's an unusual day, and nothing should surprise me. My brother stands a little to the side but I see he's spotted the reptile at the same time as I. We rush over to the animal but it quickly gets away from us, across many bushes, brooks, and other uneven terrain, yet it always remains in sight. Soon he's reached the paved road that runs below the village.

An army vehicle is parked there, one of those tracked conveyances the interior of which can't be seen through any window. The lizard enters the vehicle, then a few seconds later comes out again holding a gun. He starts firing at us. We flee; when we stop in the recess of a valley from which we can no longer see the deadly device, my brother says, breathing heavily:

"He wants me dead. It's the same lizard whose tail I cut off once, remember? Wait for me here, I'm going to see if he intends to keep chasing us. If he has quieted down, I'll ask him to forgive me. And you, all you need to do is keep watching your trap and be on your guard, you never know what might happen."

He leaves, slipping through the bushes the same way he came earlier. Soon I've lost sight of him. The cold around me intensifies and the snow on the mountain no longer reflects any sun. Suddenly everything grows dimmer, more threatening—the clouds that just before resembled fine linen flapping in the breeze assume combative shapes, the cold that was merely tickling changes into a stinging whip, and the barren trees with their rigid branches are reminders of their skeletal nature.

When my brother returns, his belly and chest are spattered with blood but he walks as if nothing is wrong. Not until he's quite close to me, do I realize how deep his wounds are. I help him sit down underneath the fig tree with its black fruit and then I run off to the village.

The distance seems longer than usual to me. Furthermore, the village is surrounded by a barbed-wire fence and I can't find the opening. When I manage to go in, I notice there's no one in the djemaâ or in any of the houses. I need to send for the men in the fields. I have to run in all directions to get some information, climb over walls, cross rivulets only to come up with a total of two individuals.

"Hurry up," I order them, "the women have already helped me make a stretcher."

"You really think that'll do any good?" one of the men answers. "In the time it took you to go for help, you really think your brother stayed alive just waiting for you?"

"We'll come with you," the other one says, "but only so that one day you won't complain about our ingratitude or accuse us of being responsible for a disaster we have nothing to do with."

Luckily, the distance that separates us from Bouharoun seems less long than when I was going in the other direction. I run until I'm gasping for breath, urging the two men behind me to keep up. When I get to Bouharoun, having completely lost the villagers from sight—perhaps they changed their mind and turned around—I find a skeleton leaning against the trunk of the fig tree with its purplish black fruit….

*

We leave the hammam very early in the morning. Above the low mountains the light is yellow and higher in the sky it's red. We stop in a café, but I barely feel the magic charm I felt in those chairs in Boubras. The smell of coffee that floats around the cramped place is, of course, very nice but it can't reduce the oppressive sadness I've been carrying inside me since I woke up. Rabah Ouali exchanges a few words with the manager and then we go into the town.

"We're going to see someone who'll show us the tomb," Rabah Ouali says.

We ask the way once and then come to a low house, almost as low as the homes in my village. Rabah Ouali knocks on a rickety wooden door and a few moments later a man comes out; he's small in stature and very old. He speaks with Rabah Ouali for quite a while and then, from what I understand, asks us in for coffee. Rabah Ouali refuses and the old man goes back inside.

"He says he helped to bury a certain number of Muslim fighters who fell under the bullets of the occupying army. But he doesn't remember every one of them. He has a few grave sites in mind that he'll show us."

The old man comes back out, dressed in a brown burnoose. I notice one of his eyes looks like blood-streaked spit and am surprised I didn't see that disability before. An immense feeling of pity sinks its roots into me, for I've always considered eyes to be the part of the body that best expresses life. Now I understand the old man's interest in the dead—he must feel so close to them.

It's still relatively cool. We go to where our donkey is tied up. When we get there Rabah Ouali unwinds his headscarf and completes his morning prayers. Then, with the old man leading us, we leave the town.

We walk and every brilliant shade of ochre, red, and white of the earth, the sand, and the mountains come rushing to meet us. Accompanied by five or six dogs, a man ahead of us drives a huge herd of sheep in a slow, tight flow. I've never seen so many sheep together.

We climb and the green and white hillocks come closer. I realize that the spots of green we saw from below, dwarf-like trees and bushes, are in reality much farther apart. This is very arid land.

Gently a hot, unpleasant wind begins to blow. For a moment it shrouds every bright color with grimy dust. Our old guide suddenly stops, looks around indecisively, then signals a shepherd who's nearby.

The two men and Rabah Ouali talk for a minute and then we take the spade and pickax from the bag. The moment of truth has come. My heart starts to beat very fast, my innards are painfully knotting up. I've always loved digging earth. But under different circumstances—to pull young rabbits from their holes.

Da Rabah digs and I remove the earth. Fortunately, the soil isn't hard. A mixture of ochre soil and sand crumbles beneath the pickax. When the hot wind begins to blow harder, it whips the earth into our faces where it sticks to our sweat.

I fling shovels full, non-stop, and my head begins to turn. I tell myself it's all a dream. Perhaps the continuation of the one last night. The sun beating our head, the blinding glitter of the stone, the pit growing ever deeper before my eyes, the sheep scattered like small clouds below us, the old man with his injured face speaking a language I don't know, it all seems totally unreal to me. And with pounding heart, my arms moving outside of me like helixes that I watch as they turn, I wait for the dream to vanish, wait for all that's real to me, for my tangible environment to reappear—the village's djemaâ with its old men, the tall green mountains with their glimpse of the sea, the destructive herds of goats, and the games dictated by the seasons.

But the grave is hopelessly present, becoming

steadily deeper. Suddenly Da Rabha's pickax hits something, it echoes feebly. He starts to dig again but more carefully this time, loosening the earth by hand. The one-eyed old man and I are bent over the grave. My distraught heart is in my throat, beating madly, keeping me from breathing. Slowly everything drains from me—head, lungs, heart; only my lower abdomen turns into the refuge for a nervous mass that painfully pounds and throbs. Then everything disintegrates into empty numbness. A bone appears, followed by another, and the skull rewards us with grinding teeth. Da Rabah takes the skull in both hands, then rises and looks at us. One of the teeth in the upper jaw is different from the others. Da Rabah scratches it with one finger—it's silver.

We remain silent for a moment.

"Your brother never had a silver tooth as far as I know!"

"No," I confirm.

Then he looks at the old man who shows him his good eye. The guide hastens to reassure us:

"There's another grave, a little further up. We buried two of the faithful that day. Each of them at the exact same place where he fell."

When he sees the unspeakable agony my face shows, Rabah Ouali translates for me.

We rest for a moment, then pack our tools. The donkey had found an auspicious bunch of thyme and refuses to let go of it. With all our strength we push him toward the land and the bare stones on the higher level, while his moist eyes keep looking back.

The day starts to become downright blistering. Around us nothing but stunted trees, stingy with their sap and shade. Silently we climb toward the gentle mountain top. Suddenly the old man stops, places his cane on a small hillock. From his gestures and words I understand he thought the grave was quite a lot higher up. Nevertheless, we decide to check. This time the old man insists on helping. There are three of us now taking turns with the shovel and the pickax. I thought the air would get cooler as we ascended, but these mountains are different from ours, and it feels as if we've merely come closer to the sun.

We dig with less reverence and caution. All we're asking now is to get this over with, to exhume the ubiquitous, mischievous skeleton, and to secure him firmly inside our bag, to be done with it once and for all.

The mound has become flat, then hollow, the pile of earth on the side is swelling. Rabah Ouali grunts. From exhaustion or rage? His face suddenly has an enigmatic expression, a blend of astonishment, curiosity, and doubt. In a frenzy he begins to dig up the soil. And I, too, am open-mouthed— at the feet of Da Rabah lies an animal skeleton. A dog, a jackal? No doubt, a shepherd must have wanted to reward the services of an extraordinary dog with such a reverent grave.

This time the old guide is not as disappointed as before. For him the discovery here is a confirmation, gives greater weight to his memories— our skeleton lies much higher up, as he thought.

We go up in soundless bad temper. The donkey follows all by himself without having to be pulled or pushed. Ali Amaouche's proud beast is unrecognizable. He's lost the bearing of that well looked-after animal he was. With his disheveled mane, his dangling tongue, his damp nostrils, he seems to have surrendered to the same inevitability that weighs upon us, and he drags on, his ears low, without even trying to comprehend. Ever since we dragged him away from his clump of thyme he's known that the worst of things can happen.

When we come to the last mound of earth, we sit down to catch our breath. Rabah Ouali is now in no rush at all to start digging. He puts the water flask close by and starts chatting with the old man. The donkey has found a humble bit of greenery—and has gone off, taking the tools with him. I, too, am beginning to lose interest in this chore; all I ask is a tiny spot of shade to protect my head.

My two companions look very spirited; they must be telling each other things that aren't sad at all since Rabah Ouali suddenly forgets himself and erupts in a loud burst of laughter. Ashamed and remorseful he looks in my direction, then observes an embarrassed silence. As if to make amends, he gets up, goes over to the donkey and gets our tools. And the digging begins again.

This time we work calmly—even serenely, or so it seems to me. There is the crushing sun but, above all, there is the certainty we have the right skeleton at last. So we want to savor it slowly and, by delaying it, have the pleasure of seeing this certainty take shape. But when Rabah Ouali kneels down to dislodge the first bones with his fingers, all my blood surges back to my heart and face, my temples begin to pound and my ears are buzzing. Feet together, I burrow deep into unfathomable anguish. Will the spell of weakness I'd feared so much at first, from which I thought I'd been delivered, now seize me after all?

I watch, my heart beating to the breaking point. There, down below, is the skeleton, indifferent to our emotions and fatigue. The half-open jaws seem to taunt us, smile at us. My brother, so reticent in life, turns out to have a smiling skeleton!

4

We now have the bones. They clatter like coins every time the donkey stumbles or has to tackle a steep path. The last cicadas and sad-sounding larks keep us company in these quiet fields, scorched by the August month. Only the evening coolness offers a balm for the burns of the route back home.

It's always exciting to leave when you don't know what to expect. But the return is a letdown. I never would have thought I could be gone from my village for so long, but we've hardly left Bordj es-Sbaâ when I see it before me, austere and unchanging, as if I'd already arrived. Having discovered other villages and even a few towns, I now realize our village really is a prison. The world is huge and some people are happy living in it. Why then keep believing all those old men who insist that guardian saints are protecting our land? Reject the protective saints! Why don't they give us more to eat, let us have better clothes? Yet, they're legion—Sidi M'hamed and his two sons; Sidi Abbou who was born in the fifth century; Sidi Mahrez with the golden belt; and Sidi Yahia, who protects the coastline. But their first vocation, I feel, is being torturer rather than saint; all they do is hamper our desires and actions, prevent us from stretching our limbs and raising our voices. At best they're guardians of an oppressive respectability.

Throughout a boring trek I brood over such reflections, which forbid me to see this mission as a triumphant return; a mission accomplished for the benefit of family and death, twin sisters, the dread of which tethers any desire inside us.

What favor did we do my brother by bringing him back with us? What really matters more to us, I believe, is burying him a second time—and still deeper in the earth—so that he'll never again get it into his head to trouble our peace and our good conscience. It's as if we weren't entirely sure he was really dead if we didn't have the new, reassuring grave within sight.

I wonder if my brother would have consented to this "move' had he been able to give us his own point of view. He was so comfortable there, lying right across from Mount Dirah in that denuded earth, naked as eternity! And here we are, taking him back, captive, his bones tightly fastened, back to the village he certainly never liked.

When he left that night of vital decisions, he knew—and I, too, was quite sure of it—that he was off on a journey of such importance he'd never return from it. But a family's resolve is more harmful than all the legions of hell put together! A family harasses you while you're alive, multiplies its restrictions on you, gags you and, once it's pushed you toward the grave, it claims draconian rights over your skeleton. Find me a land where they cannot freely dispose of your bones as they see fit. You die thinking you're leaving behind inconsolable parents, while in reality they are insatiable vultures chasing after your bones as if to extract the last bit of marrow from them. Strange country! On the one hand, they venerate the dead excessively as if to justify the life that had been made so impossible for the living, and, on the other, they exhume them to verify that nothing else can be squeezed out of them before burying them a second time, burying them in deeper ground where even memory can't find them again.

The past few months have been extraordinarily revealing—they've bared the human soul, thrown all forms of greed and stench out into the street, speeded up time like a frenzied clock.

As we move along, one field after another has been destroyed by the heat. The summer has only one smell now—that of an inextinguishable fire sizzling with grasses and insects. Shriveled beneath their straw hats, the few peasants we meet look like charred tree stumps. You'd think they have just a few more steps left in them before they'll collapse like the insects whose crumbly remains you find on tree bark and under stone.

Our return is a return without glory despite the precious booty. The only thing that weighs us down is our exhaustion, the rest barely touches us. All the assaults made on my body during the journey form a compact block that rivets my limbs and neck. I used to have similar lethargies before, a similar yearning to rest and stretch when in the summer I'd find refuge in my Uncle Ahmed's house. He had an alarm clock that ticked doggedly in the perfect silence and emptiness of the very white walls where an equally silent, fat cat would lounge around. Are there any mute cats? In any event, I never did hear that one meow. As far as I know my Uncle Ahmed is the only person in the village who owns an alarm clock. In addition, he has no children. Which makes him doubly odd. Surely that's why his house is so clean and quiet. People think it's a cursed house, that the evil spirit alone roams inside, for they've been taught to believe that "angels only visit homes that are joyous with the wailing of newborn babies". Perhaps my uncle himself believes the same thing. But he has never let on, for he's very proud, has a nervous and brittle temperament, and the most ostentatious villagers prefer to have nothing to do with him. He is actually very kind and very generous—I often had the chance to discover this when in the summer I'd go hide out in the quiet of his snow-white house. Once a question came to me—why won't he repudiate that wife of his who won't give him any children? Among our people, sterile women are soon sent back to their families. Maybe that's the cause of the villagers' animosity toward him—why doesn't he respect the basic rule that preserves the continuous infusion of new blood into the group. But he couldn't care less about the villagers. Because he knows how to make countless things with his own hands he's never asked anyone for any favors. It's usually the others who seek him out. Then he agrees to help, although grumbling, thereby spoiling many opportunities for people to express their appreciation and gratitude to him.

But my uncle is not unhappy. I even realize now that he has certain privileges, among them being absolved from having to search for bones. He's not bothered by troublesome skeletons that might haunt his sleep or make him run, always be on the move. Despite his everlasting bad temper and the fear he instills in others, he may well be the village's true sage. Because we're related, he was the obvious person to accompany me instead of Rabah Ouali. But he never seemed to take this skeleton business too seriously.

On the way back we passed through the same cities and villages but indifferently and without hurrying. Our eyes and our will, so excited when we left, are no longer inspired by the thirst to see new things and the wish to fulfill a solemn mission. We didn't stop anywhere for more than an hour. Just enough time to buy bread and fruit. We did everything we could to avoid our peers, as if the bone seekers we were when we departed had turned into bone robbers. During the trip, I once caught myself thinking that the bones in our bag might be those of a stranger whose true parents could come after us to retrieve what was theirs. I wanted to share my fears with Rabah Ouali and ask him to quicken the pace so no one could catch up with us. But the weather didn't inspire any urge to run. We're caught by the vertical sun and our legs seem shackled like those of animals you want to keep a close eye on.

Our people say that when someone doesn't react to events, God will have him reborn as a donkey in the hereafter. Surely that's a harsh condition. But in our present situation I see no difference at all between our donkey and ourselves. He's carrying the load, but the true weight of the skeleton is on our shoulders and in our heads. No matter how hard I try to think of something else, of the mountains emerging ahead of us, of the larks fusing with the stones, of the approaching village, my mind won't stop churning and grinding bones like a tireless mill. And Da Rabah, quieter than when we left, doesn't seem to be preoccupied with anything more cheerful.

The journey seems to have aged him by several years. Hearing bones clatter for days on end, makes you wonder whether there's still any flesh left on your own bones. I know death doesn't concern me. But Da Rabah must look at that differently. There's no doubt that in the pile of bones our hands and our imagination shuffled through, he saw his own skeleton being jumbled and then rearranged by the whims of time, a skull caught between kneecaps and stray shoulder blades that just came to rest on the pelvis. He certainly did see that skeleton. Disjoined from itself as surely he will be one day. Once he asked me pointblank, just like that:

"Do you think death is a decent individual?"

I really didn't know what to say to that, because first you must believe that death is, indeed, a person. He recognizes my embarrassment and continues:

"Some things are difficult for us to understand, we're just poor creatures made of mud. Take Azraïn, for example, the torturer with the club who beats the souls of the damned, do you know he's an angel? Yes, indeed, like all the other angels who watch over us with more than maternal deference. In God's established order so many things are confusing! That's why I wonder whether death might not be a

decent individual. You think that contradicts with
the task he must accomplish? Well, not so, not at
all. I imagine death coming to us like every other
guest of God. He wouldn't agree to do anything that
might attract special attention. He'd sit down with
the master of the house, on a mat, a sheepskin or
a cushion. He would have coffee, very informally.
Then, right in the middle of a conversation, he would
tell you most unpretentiously: "I am death." And
not to scare you beyond measure: "Oh, I'm not in
too much of a hurry. Take your time packing your
bags, go say goodbye to the people dear to you. It's
a journey like any other, it's just that you don't come
back."

Rabah Ouali stops talking. I know he'll be silent
for a long time. From the depths he's just dragged up
an idea that's obsessed him for days.

We've come to the village of Ifergane. It sits
perched high up on the mountain among rocks larger
than its houses. The wadi's bed down below has a few
patches of water left. They shimmer in the sun like
mirrors. This is the wadi that runs into the Azerzour
Wadi, very close to us, where it comes out into the
sea.

It is our last night outdoors. We stop at dusk,
much earlier than usual, near a big olive tree whose

foliage forms a fine, natural rooftop.

We unsaddle the donkey and go down to the wadi. The water, green and transparent, reveals a sandy bottom. The evening light is soft and lackluster. I roll up my pants and get into the water. A delightful sense of cool comes up from my feet, goes up my spine and makes me shiver a little. The last bird songs make place for the intermittent cries of insects and frightened or amorous reptiles. The green water meanders gently between my calves. Tomorrow, we'll see the sea close the horizon with a blue curtain.

Had it not been night and had we looked hard, we might have been able to see our village. But I really don't need to see it at all; I know the village is up there, unchanged in our absence, with its carefully walled up secrets and its gaze cold as stone that no summer ever brightens. It will be up there, always opposing the bewilderment of those who question with the same silence, a stubborn, ancient silence that damages wounds.

Traveling such distances and crossing so many villages reveal strange and difficult things about your fellowmen and about yourself. Without a word Rabah Ouali and I lie down under the olive tree as new luminous particles explode in the sky. Even the very natural joy of coming home after a long absence feels strange to us.

How many dead will actually come home to the village tomorrow? I'm sure that the deadest one of us is not my brother's skeleton, rattling inside the bag with unfeigned pleasure. Persistent in his efforts and his braying, the donkey is perhaps the only living being our small convoy is bringing back.

16 January 1983

DIÁLOGOS BOOKS
DIALOGOSBOOKS.COM